MY GIRL

Crazy Little Thing Called Love

A touching, heartwarming story that takes your breath away.

Characters that will have you feeling so many emotions. It deals with family, misunderstandings, ranch life, horses, life long love and of course Pumpkin the cat.

Tony and Sophia's story had me laughing, crying and a bit frustrated with them at times. To me that is good writing when I can be moved to so many emotions while reading . The story is so good, I couldn't put it down.

— B

Hold 'Em

This story is Laugh out loud funny at times and heartwarmingly tender at others! Both Matt and Cassandra have suffered a lot growing up, have overcome a lot and seem to have such high hopes for their respective futures. But first they just need to get through one measly week without killing each other! But can they? I can't recommend this novella highly enough - it's so worth 1-clicking then snuggling up on the couch to just get lost in and ENJOY!

— BARBARA

MY GIRL

GAMBLING HEARTS- BOOK 3

JACQUIE BIGGAR

WAVEFRONT PUBLISHING

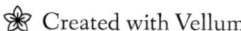

For my Family
My daughter is the greatest gift my husband ever gave me.
Love, always

Children are the world's greatest healer.

— JACQUIE BIGGAR

INTRODUCTION

Sometimes, the right decision isn't the easiest one to make

Trish Sylvester knows her family and when they accept a week long stay at a rustic dude ranch, she is concerned- especially since it's at her ex's home.

Aaron is overjoyed at the opening of his family's guest ranch, until he learns their first guest is his ex-girlfriend, her parents--and a fiancé.

And that isn't the only surprise.

Aaron Shaughnessy reined Dickens to a halt on a ridge overlooking the southern boundary of the family ranch, the valley spread before him. A shimmering ribbon of water slowly meandered while Charolais and Black Angus grazed on grass deep enough to tickle their bellies. Birds and butterflies flitted from the broad backs of the cattle to wildflowers dotting the landscape and back again—winged soldiers riding great steeds. The cool breeze caressing his skin was a pleasant change from the overly warm day. He'd been riding on Balmoral land for hours, checking fence and mending barbwire. He was tired and sore but satisfied with his accomplishments.

He patted the Andalusian's satiny gray neck. "You worked hard today, big guy. Time for dinner?" The horse's nod jangled the bit and bridle. His long black mane tickled Aaron's hand at rest on his thigh. "Okay, let's go then."

With little more than a touch of the reins, the gelding wheeled and trotted toward home, his stomach's inner compass infallible.

"Matt sure has you trained well." Aaron chuckled. He'd originally been against the horse breeding program, but three years later it was proving to be a viable business venture. It figured—everything his brother touched turned to gold.

Or gambling chips.

As wagers go, the way Matt met his wife, Cassandra, had definitely paid off. Cass enriched their family with her quick wit and kindness. She'd been a good influence on his impetuous sister, Sophia, as well, though the high-class advertising executive that came home from New York City last year bore little resemblance to the kid sister he'd tormented as a child. He still couldn't figure out how she'd convinced his private brother to open the homestead up as a dude ranch. Hell, he wasn't sure he liked it himself and he was the social one.

On the way down from the ridgeline, he stopped to check on the rock berms he'd constructed to conserve water for the land. The pipe sticking out of the hill poured into a five-hundred-gallon reservoir that in turn fed the streams and ponds in this section, along with the hacienda. They'd also implemented a plan to rid the farm of invasive plants, such as the Ashe juniper, and scatter the seeds for native grasses. Slowly but surely the drought-ridden land was making a recovery.

Matt thought he was wasting his time.

Dickens tossed his head.

"Yeah, me too, boy. He has a way of cutting a guy off at the knees, doesn't he?" Much as he loved this land, Aaron had a feeling his days here were numbered. He couldn't keep butting heads with his brother without it destroying the family.

They rode into the courtyard just as a group of five trotted in from the west. Stark white cowboy hats, starched shirts and stiff jeans proclaimed them city folk almost as much as the rigid postures and mixture of trepidation and excitement in their expressions. Riding a horse for the first time was a thrill, but it came with a price tag. They'd be wise to make use of the hot tub later —after grooming their animals, of course. This guest ranch operated on the premise, *Balmoral; for a full Cowboy Experience.* Their visitors paid good money to earn those sore muscles.

Aaron nodded to a smiling Sophia and was about to guide Dickens around the crowd when a sudden cry caught his attention. A woman—riding at the back of the group—fought her agitated horse. She yanked on the reins, arms flailing as the animal snorted and reared before sidestepping sharply away from the fountain in the center of the courtyard. Spooked by the commotion, the other horses whinnied, bumping against each other and creating instant pandemonium for their riders.

Sophia grasped the reins of a bay ridden by a screaming older woman and narrowly missed getting knocked off her own mount in the process. Aaron nudged Dickens with his knees and leaned forward in the saddle. The animal leaped across the distance, ears back and sides quivering. As soon as they were near enough, he launched from his saddle onto the back of the piebald carrying the first distraught woman. He wrapped his arms around her waist to hold her in the saddle and grabbed for the reins before she dropped them. The horse, thoroughly panicked, took off at a gallop, shoes clattering on the cobblestones. He kicked up dirt as he veered up one of the trails. Short of sawing on the poor animal's mouth, the only thing Aaron could do was let him ride out his terror.

Powerful hindquarters bunched under his legs. He tightened his grip on the trembling woman, his seat precarious on the bay's rump. If either of them fell now, they could be trampled. Her hat had fallen off in the scuffle and a long stream of blond hair prevented him from seeing where they were going.

"Hang on," he shouted, and thought he heard her sharp retort, "No kidding." *Great, a smart ass.*

Slow and easy, bit by bit, he hauled back on the reins, giving the horse a chance to get over his fright. By the time he settled down, they were a couple of miles from home. Aaron moved the reins to his left hand and braced his fingers on the cantle—uncomfortably close to the stranger's shapely behind sheathed in dark blue denim.

4

He pushed off the horse's rump, landing with a soft thud in the dirt. The animal side-stepped nervously, but the fight had gone out of him. The black and white patched head hung, his neck flecked with sweaty foam, sides heaving.

"What did you do to my horse?"

Huh? Aaron squinted at the shadowy image, her appearance hidden within the brilliant rays of the sun. He didn't need to see her to know she was annoying, though. He gathered the reins, moved to the piebald's head and rubbed his forehead. "It's okay, big guy. Something freaked you out back there, didn't it? If you had an experienced rider—"

"I *am* experienced, Aaron Shaughnessy, and well you know it."

That voice. Aaron's teeth clenched as his stomach did a nose-dive. "Trish? What are you doing here?"

His ex-girlfriend gracefully swung her leg over the horse's back and dropped to the ground at his side. Brilliant sea green eyes mocked his obviously shocked expression. "Why do I get the feeling you aren't happy to see me?"

S ophia scrambled to bring the jittery horses under control and smiled her relief when Tony rode into the fray to help. Her husband of nine months liked to keep a watchful eye on her, and at moments like these she was grateful.

"Whoa. Whoa, there," he said, nudging his mount next to Mr. Sylvester's.

The older man, far from looking appreciative, snarled and threw him the reins. "If this is how you run a business, no wonder it's failing."

Sophia's heart plunged. She'd looked forward to having the Sylvester's out to the ranch after a disastrous end to the business relationship with their son last year. Now, it was all falling apart.

She forced a smile. "Don't worry, my brother will keep your daughter safe. I really don't understand how this happened. Matt is an experienced trainer. These horses are normally so calm children ride them."

"That's hardly a recommendation—considering." The third person in their guest party sat his saddle with confidence. He'd been introduced as Trish Sylvester's fiancé, which begged the question; what was he doing here instead of seeing to her protection?

"Kyle, be a dear and help me off of this, this... beast," Mrs. Sylvester said, her voice papery thin. He looked startled but dismounted to give her a hand.

Mr. Sylvester eyed his wife with disgust before following suit. He turned to Sophia and ignored Tony completely. "My daughter had better return without harm, or I will sue you into the ground." He grasped his wife's hand and stomped toward the hacienda.

Sophia frowned at Kyle's smirk. "Aren't you concerned about your fiancée?" He hadn't shown the slightest inclination to go after her.

He shrugged. "She's been on a horse before. Maybe you haven't noticed, but her family is rather melodramatic. She'll be fine."

Tony didn't even try to hide his opinion of the other man. He shook his head and gathered the reins of all the horses. "I'd better get these animals taken care of—you coming?" He looked at Sophia, his blue eyes cool.

She hesitated, torn between duty to her guest and the urge to walk away before she said something she'd regret. "Would you like to help us groom the horses?" she asked, the politeness Gran had instilled in her winning out.

Kyle laughed. "I'll give it a pass. Besides, that's what the staff gets paid to do, isn't it?" He nodded toward Tony.

Sophia bristled. "Tony happens to be my husband," she snapped. Decision made. She strode to her cowboy and planted a kiss on his mouth. "Let's get out of here, something stinks."

Tony grinned. "Yes, ma'am."

She glanced over her shoulder. "I trust you can find your way to the hacienda, Mr. Lane? Consuela will have dinner ready by five."

"Five?" he asked incredulously. "And what do you expect us to do for the rest of the evening?"

"I have an idea or two," Tony said under his breath.

"Shh," she whispered, stifling the urge to giggle. He made her feel like the teenage girl who'd first fallen for the handsome young man her father had rescued from a bad situation. "We rise early on the ranch, you'll want to get some rest," she said aloud to the annoying guest they were leaving behind.

When she'd planned a dude ranch with so much excitement, she'd figured Matt for a hard sell, not the people who paid them to stay. This was harder than she expected. Maybe she'd made a mistake.

"Stop it," Tony ordered and used his free arm to draw her next to his whipcord lean body. "I can practically hear that sweet head of yours second-guessing yourself and believe me, guys like that are not worth the time."

She burrowed under his arm and hugged him close. "What if he's right? Matt hated my idea, and Aaron—"

He stopped and turned her toward him. "Soph, it's a good plan. If it saves the ranch, your brothers are going to bow at your feet. I'm serious," he said when she shook her head. "Stop doubting yourself, honey. I believe in you. Now you just have to learn to trust your judgement." He tipped her chin up and gently kissed her lips. "Come on. If we hurry, we might have time for a nap before dinner."

Her pulse kicked up its heels, well aware of what he meant by *nap*. How did she get so lucky? Tony was everything she could ever have longed for in a husband—and soon-to-be father. She'd been saving the news for a special occasion, and today felt right. Laughing, overcome with joy, she tugged on her lover's hand. "What are you waiting for?"

How DID she get so lucky?

Trish stared at the golden Adonis at her side and cursed the ground her parents walked upon. They'd promised—*promised*—Aaron would *not* be at the ranch for the duration of their stay. Thank goodness she had Kyle.

"Surprised?" she taunted, while inside butterflies swirled giddily. She placed a hand over her tummy to quell the fluttering.

"It's been a long time," he said, his gaze stripping her bare.

She stiffened but forced herself not to react. Not an easy task. Aaron Shaughnessy wasn't a man to ignore. "How have you been?"

He chuckled but the humor never came near his eyes. "Do you care?" He shook his head. "Never mind, it doesn't matter. What are you doing here, Trish?"

Here it was; the million-dollar question. She suddenly ached to tell him the truth. To talk, really talk, like they used to for hours and hours—about anything and everything. She'd known him better than his own family.

It had been her with the secrets.

She turned away on the pretext of patting her horse's neck. "At least he didn't throw me, that's good news."

"Don't turn your back on me." Aaron grasped her shoulder and swung her around, startling the gelding into sidestepping.

They struck sparks off each other—always had. A thrill ran down her spine, but she viciously tamped it down and broke free. "Still the same, I see. It's your way or the highway." She'd never been so alive as when she and Aaron had dated. A hard ball of regret burned in her chest.

He raised his hands and took a step back, giving them both some space. "Look... I don't know what game you're playing, but I don't want you here. I'll take you to the hacienda, and you can pack your bags. Hell, I'll even call you a cab—after that I don't ever want to see you again. We clear?"

Well, she'd known this wasn't going to be easy.

"You might want to talk to your sister about that. She's the one who invited us."

3

The ride back to the compound was made in grim silence. Aaron led the way and kept a firm grip on the other horse's lead while Trish had a stranglehold on the pommel. Tempted to trot and increase her discomfort, he couldn't bring himself to be that rude.

That was her forte.

The sun lay on the horizon in a golden-red globe by the time they arrived. *Tía* Consuela rushed out of the house to greet them, long skirts swishing in the dust.

"There you are. I worried you wouldn't find the sweet miss," she called. Her smile revealed deep dimples in her leathery cheeks. "That barn cat has to go."

Trish surprised him by hopping out of the saddle as though she was a seasoned rider. "What cat?" she asked, leaning over to straighten her pant legs.

Aaron jerked his gaze away from her mile-long legs

and dismounted. He ground-tied their horses and bent to give his aunt a kiss. "How are you feeling today? What did the doctor say?"

Consuela patted his cheek. "Tut, tut, my dear boy. I told you not to worry. I'm going to be just fine." She turned to Trish. "I'm so sorry, Miss, it was my fault. If I hadn't started feeding the stray cat that showed up a couple of weeks ago, this would never have happened."

That explained the streak of black he thought he'd seen as he rode into the courtyard earlier. The cat must have spooked the horses, causing Trish to lose control.

"*Tía*," he scolded. "You know Matt doesn't like cats."

She frowned. "And why not? Your sainted grandmother always had a cat in the house." She dabbed at her eyes with the corner of her apron. "I miss her every day."

He hugged her petite body. "Me too, Aunty. Me Too." It was little more than a year since Madeline, the family matriarch, passed and they were still finding their way without her.

Trish cleared her throat and Aaron let his aunt go to glare in her direction.

She lifted her chin. "Thank you for riding to my rescue—though I could have managed just fine on my own—I'm going to head in and get cleaned up now." Her gaze warmed as it moved to Consuela. "My room is beautiful. Sophia sang your praises for so long, I'm glad we had the opportunity to visit. I'm just sorry we can't stay longer."

Consuela's brows furrowed. "But miss, you're booked

for a week. Sophia planned a hayride, branding exhibition, and even a Halloween barn dance. Are you sure you can't stay?"

Aaron cursed under his breath. His sister had gone to a lot of effort to make the Sylvesters' visit a success and he knew damn well Trish was leaving because he'd demanded it.

He was caught between a rock and a hard place.

"Stay," he muttered and stared at a gap near the top of the fountain. He'd have to find that stray cat before Matt did. Maybe one of the ranch hands could take the poor critter. His brother barely accepted Sophia's ginger cat, he'd never take in another.

"I'm sorry, can you repeat that? Because I thought you just finished telling me—"

"How beautiful the farm is this time of year," he finished hastily.

She gave him a disbelieving glare from slitted green eyes. "Well, how can I say no then?"

Tía Consuela was the only one happy with the change of events. She clapped her hands together and grasped Trish's elbow. "Now you stay, come in and sample my fresh-made empanadas. The children, they love them."

Aaron scowled as he watched the women enter the house. He had a feeling he was going to be sorry he'd given in to his aunt's wishes. He was still bitter about the way Trish had broken things off between them last year after the deal he'd been working on with her brother failed. It had seemed like one negated the other. He hadn't wanted to think that of her, but when she'd refused all his calls he'd been left with no other option.

And now she was back.

He gathered the reins and led the horses toward the stables. The cavernous whitewashed building had pens for forty animals, many of them poking their heads over the stall doors as he entered the dim interior. The Thoroughbred-Andalusian breeding program had created healthy foals and already they were receiving handsome offers for the yearlings. Matt planned to buy new breeding stock from the proceeds of the sales and continue to build their herd into some of the most sought-after jumpers in Texas.

The low murmur of voices drew to a halt as he neared the tack room. He tipped the scruffy white cowboy hat to the back of his head, nodded absently to Rico who held a beat-up leather ledger and a carpenter's pencil in his hands, and waited for Matt to join him in the corridor.

"What's up?"

Matthew waved a hand, pointing up and down the aisle. "Work's up. You know, that thing you like to avoid."

Aaron caught Rico's raised brow and his ears grew hot. He didn't know why, but his brother had the ability to make him feel like a chastised child with little more than a glance. He'd known better than to try idle chit-chat with the lord-of-the-manor.

Dickens butted his head between them and gently blew on Aaron's cheek. Aaron gave the satiny neck a rub, grateful for the sign of affection. At least one creature in his life loved him. Sometimes, he figured he was better off hanging out with the animals than trying to please his family.

"Whatever, man. Look, I need to get these two taken care of, so if you're finished—" He tightened his grip on the trailing reins and continued his journey down the barn to Dickens' stall. His horse nickered and entered the twelve-by-twelve room on his own, heading straight for the water pail.

Aaron tied off the horse Trish had ridden to an iron ring mounted outside the stall, then turned to follow Dickens, only to pull up short when his brother passed him with a rectangle bale of hay. He deposited it on the floor near the feed trough, cut the cords holding it together, and reached out to pat the big horse's flank.

"I'm sorry," he said, moving out of the way as the gelding dove into the feed. "I'd forgotten you were going out to ride fence today. Had a few things come up and I guess I took it out on you. Want a hand with the grooming?"

Okay, who is this guy and what did he do with my brother?

It wasn't like him to apologize or offer to do chores. They'd been brought up to care for the animals before themselves. Even as children, their father had brought step stools out to the barn so they could learn to curry and brush their ponies. And later he'd taught them to use hoof picks, check for swelling, and care for their own tack.

16

When Dad, their mother and Grandpa Joseph died in a small plane crash, Grandma Madeline had taken over caring for the three kids. Not for the first time, he wondered what she'd gone through losing a husband, son and daughter-in-law in one shocking swoop while gaining sole custody of small children and a five thousand acre working ranch. No wonder she'd been a legend in these parts.

"Sure." He nodded toward the mare standing beyond the doorway. "One of Sophia's guests ended up on a runaway today. She handled it, don't worry," he said when Matt jerked. "I went after her and she seemed just fine. Nothing a spa day can't cure for the city girl." He wasn't about to share *who* the escapee had been. Plenty of time for that clusterfudge when his sister was around to explain herself.

Matt heaved a heavy sigh and reached for the curry comb resting on the ledge. "I don't know why I let her talk me into this harebrained idea. Our ancestors would turn over in their graves if they knew." He waited until Aaron removed the saddle and blanket, then ran the comb in a circular motion over the horse's back. The dappled gray coat rippled beneath his touch.

Aaron eyed him over Dickens' neck as he used a brush to straighten the mane. "Don't you think you're being melodramatic? Give it a chance. If it works out, it'll be the solid source of income the ranch needs. Especially since you shot down my plans last year." He hadn't meant to say anything, but sometimes Matt's holier-than-thou attitude rankled. It wasn't like Mr. Professional Gambler didn't have a few foibles of his own, after all.

Dickens shuffled, picking up on the tension invading the room. Aaron rubbed between the velvety ears until the horse calmed. "Look, we all want what's best for the ranch."

Matt snorted.

Aaron glared at his brother. "What's that supposed to mean?"

Matt took his time answering. He finished combing his side of the horse, checked the hooves and fetlocks, then strode over to heft the saddle over his shoulder before turning to Aaron. "If you love this place as much as you profess, then why were you going to sell off your share of the ranch the minute the ink dried on the ownership papers?"

Without waiting for a reply, he stalked out of the stall and left Aaron to stew in a quagmire of his own making.

4

Trish sat at the ginormous island and watched the Shaughnessys' housekeeper buzz around the kitchen. Consuela filled a copper kettle with water from the deep farm sink before settling it to heat on a six-burner gas stove with double ovens. Then she turned to the stainless-steel refrigerator and began to haul out what seemed like a mountain of food—sliced tomatoes, cucumbers, homemade salsa, guacamole, aioli, limes and a heaping plate of empanadas.

"Would you like me to make nachos to go with this, dear?" Consuela asked, her head in the fridge.

Trish looked around, but no, she was the only other person in the room. There was already enough food to feed an army. No wonder those Shaughnessys loved their home.

"Thank you," she said. "This is great. Are you sure I can't help?"

"Oh, no, dear. You're company, after all." Consuela shut the door with a broad hip, her hands full with a large platter of chopped fruit. "Besides, I like to take care of my kids and their... friends." She smiled cheerfully and dumped the platter in front of Trish. "Eat up now, you're too thin. You need hips like mine to have healthy children, you know." She gave a little wriggle just as the kettle whistled. "Oh, there's our tea water—won't be but a moment."

Bemused, Trish plucked a juicy red grape from the tray and popped it into her mouth, savoring the sweet-tart flavor. She waited until Consuela rejoined her at the counter before asking the question preying on her mind. "So... is Aaron seeing anyone?"

Consuela's knowing grin heated Trish's cheeks.

"He's a fine-looking lad, that one." She filled the earthenware teacups and handed Trish the sugar bowl. "Just a dab to sweeten the pot, you know. Darn doctor keeps harping on my blood sugars, but a gal needs her sweets now and then." She crawled up onto one of the high stools with a grunt and sighed over her cup. "That boy hasn't had it easy, being the middle child. He feels invisible, even though his brother and sister adore him. But then, maybe you know what that's like?" Her chocolate-brown eyes met Trish's. "Your father was a bit upset when he came in earlier."

Trish set the empanada she'd been nibbling onto a napkin, her stomach knotting at the mention of her dad. When her brother, Andy, had come home with a pamphlet for the newly opened Balmoral Dude Ranch, she'd assumed he'd had a change of heart and was happy for his friend, Aaron. The suggestion to book a family getaway for autumn should have been the proverbial red flag. Her biggest mistake was in thinking her family was normal.

"He doesn't want to accept his baby girl has grown up," she said. If her tone was sardonic, she hoped the kindly maid took it for exhaustion.

Consuela patted her hand. "No father does, dear. Their instinct is to protect their cubs." She smiled and took another sip of tea, her eyes fluttering closed to fully enjoy the forbidden treat.

Or destroy them. The dark thought wormed its way into Trish's mind and grew like the plague. She'd lost count of the number of times her dad had let them down over the years.

Trish had looked forward to this trip as a way to mend the distance that had grown between her and Andy in recent years—and, if she was being honest, the possibility of seeing Aaron again.

Aaron.

A wanton thrill coursed through her veins. He'd rescued her on the runaway horse like a hero from a romance novel. She could have eventually managed to control the animal herself—it wasn't her first time on a horse—but, she wouldn't trade those minutes with Aaron for anything. Even though he'd reacted like a jerk.

"Where are my parents?" she asked, not really surprised they hadn't waited to make sure she was safe.

"In their room, I believe—your mother wasn't feeling well."

Her mother was always ill. They'd spent half their childhoods getting dragged from one medical clinic to another holistic health center. She'd missed her friends' sleepovers and even her own birthday party one year because her mother '*just didn't feel up to dealing with the stress, of it all*'.

"Oh, yes. Your young man said when you were done gallivanting—" Consuela's brows hunched up like an old woman's back, "—he would be waiting in the library."

Shoot, Kyle.

Trish hopped off the stool and took a last sip of the delicious herbal tea. "I better go find him, he must be worried," she said and avoided Consuela's kindly brown eyes. "Thank you for the delicious food. You were absolutely right, your empanadas are the best I've ever tried, and I'm from Austin. I've had my share of fantastic Mexican dishes." She was babbling now—*great*.

A scrambling of nails over the terra cotta tiles broke the awkward silence. Trish gaped at a ginger cat with a bushy tail chasing a tiny black dog in one door and out the other with a chorus of yapping.

"Was that dog bald?" she asked, not sure whether to believe her eyes.

Consuela clucked her tongue. "Those two, they never quit. The noisy one was Master Matt's hairless

Chihuahua, Chewy. He's the instigator, don't let that adorable face fool you."

Adorable wasn't quite the description Trish would have used, remembering the long pink tongue hanging out of the critter's mouth. She could more easily picture the hard-nosed Matthew Shaughnessy with a Rottweiler than the little rat who'd just run through the kitchen. But somehow, it made him more approachable. She decided her father didn't need to know about this, at least not from her. He enjoyed using whatever he perceived as a weakness against his opponents.

And make no mistake, that's what the Shaughnessys were. She needed to remember that.

"Okay, I guess I'll see you at dinner then?" she asked Consuela as she moved toward the doorway.

"Sí. Five o'clock in the main salon. Semi-formal, if you brought dress clothes. Sophia likes to keep the traditions alive—just like her grandmother, that one."

As Trish made her way toward the library in the beautiful Spanish-style villa, she reflected on the sibling heirs. Each different, yet bound to the land, and she wished for the impossible.

5

Aaron tugged off his dusty leather gloves and slapped them against his thigh as he entered the coolness of the villa. It had taken longer than expected to groom the horses—he'd found a slight swelling on the fetlock of the animal Trish had been riding. Not serious enough to call in the vet, but worrisome, nonetheless. He'd treated it with a cold-water hose bath and asked Rico to keep an eye on him. Stocking up was fairly common in horses and easily treated if caught in time. He hadn't found any bite marks or signs of abscess, though something had set the animal off and he didn't think it was a damn Halloween cat. Their horses were carefully exposed to all manner of scents and sounds—they had to be if the general public would be riding them. The last thing the ranch needed was a lawsuit on their hands.

The conversation with Matt had left a sour taste in

his mouth and he veered for the library, deciding to soak his sorrows in a glass of whiskey before dinner. Annoyance rose at the sight of a stranger—one of Sophia's guests, he assumed—sprawled out on the sofa, a drink on the table and cell phone in hand.

Aaron wasn't in the mood to play nice with the company, he'd go to his room and shower instead. He'd just started to reverse direction when the man glanced over. An immediate sense of animosity flashed between the two men, though he couldn't say why.

"Howdy," he said, heading for the fully stocked wet bar. "Long day. Thought I'd grab a drink. Refill?" He nodded toward the nearly empty drink on the table.

"Yeah, sure." The stranger rose and brought his glass to the counter. He waited for Aaron to put a conservative splash into his own glass over a bed of ice, then reached for the bottle. "Name's Kyle Lane. You work here?" He filled his glass with a two-finger shot and downed half in one swallow. "I can't believe I let myself get talked into a week in the boonies." He laughed as though it was a big joke.

Aaron frowned. Just what they needed; a drunk. "Hardly the *boonies*," he replied and forced a friendly grin though it felt more like a grimace. "We have all the amenities; satellite television, internet—though it tends to run slow in the evening—hot tub, a fully-equipped games room, daily activities, and if you really feel the need for more, Austin is only an hour away."

"Don't remind me," Kyle groused. He yanked the

loosened tie from around his neck and undid the top two buttons on his expensive-looking dress shirt. "If Trish's old man hadn't insisted, you wouldn't have caught me within a hundred yards of this place." He tossed the tie on the counter and took another slug of the whiskey before staring into the bottom of his glass. "Any idea where they hide the top shelf liquor? Figures they leave the cheap shit out for their guests."

Aaron stiffened. The jerk didn't know his alcohol from a hole in the ground. And what was that about Trish? He moved the bottle further from the other man's reach. There was nothing worse than an ugly drunk in his opinion.

"Are you a... friend of Trish Sylvester's, then?" he asked, his gut tensing for the answer, though what did he expect? She was a beautiful woman, of course she would have moved on.

Kyle snorted, his eyes glassy now that the booze had kicked in. "That's one way of putting it, yeah. We're engaged." He flashed a lop-sided grin. "I hooked a rich babe who knows how to—"

"Hey, watch your mouth." Aaron's fists clenched. He itched to knock those perfect teeth out of the asshole's mouth. What did Trish see in this guy?

Kyle backed up a couple of steps—maybe he was smarter than he looked after all—and raised his hands in the air. "Take it easy, I didn't mean anything by it. Trish is a sweet girl, I'm lucky to have her."

"You're preachin' to the choir, man." Aaron turned away, disgusted. "Trish and I go way back. You might want to find out who you're sharing confidences with next time before opening a can of worms you can't retract." He reached for the door. "By the way, I don't just work here. I'm part owner."

Kyle's eyes widened even as he swayed against the bar. Aaron shook his head. *Idiot.*

He took a steadying breath and stepped into the hall, straight into the oncoming path of his ex-girlfriend.

"Oh," she stammered, slim hands bracing against Aaron's chest. "I didn't see you there."

Aaron's senses were overwhelmed with the scent and feel of Trish. His fingers gripped her hips, the urge to tug her closer so she could feel what she did to him riding him hard. Her green eyes pulled him into their depths, seeming to make promises he knew, *knew*, she wouldn't keep. Damn it, what was it about this woman? Why couldn't he get her out of his blood?

"I met your fiancé," he said, his voice ripe with challenge. The outdoors clung to her skin; sun, flowers, and woman combining to intoxicate him more than the whiskey.

She lifted her chin, eyes narrowing. "What did you say to him, Aaron? I'd hoped we could act like adults while we're here."

Aaron laughed, his hands doing the job his heart urged him to do, forcing her to come up against his chest with a soft oomph. "Darlin', I'm definitely a man, make no mistake." He leaned down and brushed her lips, setting up a barrage of warnings through his chest. He was playing with fire, and if he wasn't careful, there was little doubt who was going to get burned. Again.

"Aaron, stop this," she murmured, though her lips parted on a sigh. "We can't..."

He lifted his head and stared at her upturned face. "Can't what? You invited yourself onto my territory and brought reinforcements. I want to know why."

She moved out of his arms. He pretended not to feel the loss.

"We needed a break from the city," she said. "Surely, you can understand that? Your sister sent an email to me highlighting the new business venture—congrats, by the way—and I thought it would be fun to come and check it out. End of story."

He eyed her nervously tucking her hair behind her ear and knew she was bluffing. The question remained; why?

"Look, Trish, whatever is going—"

"There you are," Kyle slurred from the doorframe he was plastered against. "I've been sitting here all damn afternoon. Your pops warned you..."

She hurried to his side, tucking a supporting arm around his waist. "Let's get you to your room before you fall. What possessed you to drink like this?" She glanced at Aaron and away. "Never mind, a shower will help."

Kyle grinned slyly. "Are you offering to wash my

back, sweetheart?" He too, glanced at Aaron as though to make sure his barb sank in.

It had.

"Don't forget, dinner's at five." Aaron turned on his heel and walked away before he did something he might not regret.

6

Trish wore a path in the plush green carpet covering the floor of her bedroom while waiting for Kyle to finish his shower in the room next door. She hadn't seen her parents since her return. It was heartwarming to know how much they'd worried about her safety—*not*. They'd made it clear many years ago they expected their children to accept the consequences of their actions—and learn from them. Nurturing was not a term one thought of in conjunction with Dave and Eleanor Sylvester.

She whirled at a light tap on the door, her heart tripping over itself. Aaron wouldn't come to her room, would he?

Sophia poked her head around the door and Trish stifled her disappointment.

"Hi," she said, stepping into the room. "I just wanted

to make sure you were okay after this afternoon's misadventure."

Trish smiled. Sophia had lived in New York while Trish dated Aaron. Then the Shaughnessy's grandmother's death had taken center stage and the women hadn't had the chance to get to know each other before the relationship ended, but she genuinely liked Aaron's younger sister.

"I think you should add *'Get rescued by a handsome cowboy'* to the itinerary. You'll be inundated with single ladies looking for a western romance. It would be good for business."

Sophia giggled and plopped down on the end of the bed. "You might have something there—though maybe not by Aaron. He's liable to scare our customers away."

No, not with Aaron. Trish had no right feeling the way she did, but that didn't make the murderous vein in her neck stop throbbing any faster. Just the thought of another woman in Aaron's arms...

"Hey, it was a joke. Did my brother do something to annoy you?" Sophia eyed her curiously.

Remembering the feel of his arms around her, frustration was more the term that came to mind. "Aaron was the perfect gentleman," she said and changed the subject to the real reason for the trip. "Have you thought anymore about the proposal my father outlined for you during our ride?"

Sophia dropped the slightly ditzy girlfriend pose and

donned the mantle of the successful businesswoman she'd been in New York. She crossed one shapely leg over the other and placed folded hands on her knee. "Without facts and numbers, I'm not at liberty to make a decision of that caliber. As you know, my brothers and I own equal shares in the ranch. I would have to get their approval before moving forward. I can't do that until I have a contract, in writing—"

Vexed, Trish still took a moment to admire the woman's integrity. Sophia sat on the end of the bed for all the world as though she were at a multi-national meeting wearing a power suit instead of blue jeans and a ruffled pink blouse. Unfortunately, it was Trish's job to tear that persona apart.

Tomorrow.

Just for today she wanted to pretend she was here to have a good time. "No rush," she murmured as the rattling pipes ended their musical notes and signaled Kyle's imminent arrival. "I'm sure it will all work out. I don't think I've ever been in a house like this, can you share some of the history with me?"

Sophia gave a wry grimace. "That's a polite way of saying our home is old. No, no it's okay," she said, holding up a hand when Trish tried to apologize. "You'd be right. The hacienda is over one hundred years old, built by my great-grandfather for his new bride. There've been a few additions over the years, but we tried to retain the integrity of the building."

She strode to the window with its view of the rolling hills. "A few miles from here, in a place called Hidden

Valley, there's a cabin that's near and dear to my family. Matthew and I were both married there." She turned with a mischievous smile. "I've been thinking of setting it up for destination weddings—you know, *'visit the great outdoors and get hitched while you're here.'* Maybe you could be our first guest bride?"

Trish had planned for her wedding since she was a young girl. She still had the scrapbooks she'd used after carefully cutting out the perfect dress, bouquet, flowers, venue—everything her twelve-year-old mind could dream up. And nowhere in that sacred journal would she find pictures of a back-country wedding.

Funny how perfect it sounded now.

She picked up her hairbrush and ran it needlessly through her hair before tying it back with a velvet ribbon. "I don't think I'm ready to get married," she said, fiddling with the oversized diamond on her finger.

"Um, does your fiancé know this?" Sophia asked, moving to Trish's side. "If you need to talk—"

"No. Thank you though." Trish met her empathic gaze and cursed her rambling tongue. "Put it down to bridal nerves. I'll be fine tomorrow."

Sophia took the brush from Trish's fingers and grasped her hand. "I realize we aren't buddies—yet—but my brother fell in love with you at one time and that tells me that you're someone I need to get to know better." She smiled at Trish's start of surprise. "Did you think it was a secret? My brothers don't keep much from me, I'm too nosey." She laughed.

Trish squeezed her hand before letting it go. She was beginning to hate this trip and what it was turning her into.

"You're wrong, Aaron and I were... friends, but that ended a long time ago. It was a casual relationship that ran its course. We weren't exactly compatible—I mean, he's country and I'm a city girl through and through. It never would have worked."

Sophia opened her mouth to say something but was interrupted by a banging on the door that had both women flinching.

"Hey, Trish," Kyle called out from the other side of the heavy wood panels. "Hurry up, I'm hungry. Let's hope it's healthier than the swill they've served so far."

Trish glared a hole in the door before turning to apologize to their hostess. "He's usually better than this, I'm so sorry."

Sophia shrugged it off. "Men. You can't live with them and you can't bury them in the backyard for the coyotes to find. The law frowns on that sort of thing."

They looked at each other and grinned before opening the door to an irate fiancé.

7

Aaron debated whether to skip out on the evening meal, but in the end, he turned up at the dining room just as the guests took their seats.

Matt was in his chair at the head of the table with Cassandra on his left and Trish's parents—Dave and Eleanor—on the right. Next to them, Sophia perched on the edge of her seat, chatting with the guests as her husband, Tony, looked on benevolently, his hand resting on her back. Across the table, Trish sat stiff and silent, next to her idiot boyfriend.

Which left him the seat between Trish and Cassandra. *Great.*

His sister-in-law smiled as he took his place. "Glad you could make it tonight. You rarely attend family dinners anymore."

Her chiding tone sent prickles of discomfort crawling

up his spine—or maybe that was Matt's judgmental stare. "Yeah, well, I'm sure you get along fine without me," he said, reaching for his water glass.

Trish didn't say a word, but he could feel her disapproval just the same. It was none of her business, she'd given up that right a long time ago. He switched from water to the sweating beer bottle sitting beside it. A long, cool swallow later and he had his equilibrium back—or so he thought.

"Checked the fence in the west quadrant earlier today. I thought you said it was done?" Matt frowned at the beer in his hand.

Inside, Aaron's blood began to seethe, but he'd be damned if he'd allow it to show in front of Trish and her family. He took another drink to spite his brother before leaning casually back in his chair, idly twirling a fork on the table by its tines.

"No, I'm pretty sure I said I'd done the south section and planned to get onto the west end within a few days."

Matt leaned forward, his wide shoulders stretching the seams of his dress shirt. "I needed you out west, little bro. That damn stallion made off with another three mares because the fence wasn't mended."

"The ghost stallion?" Sophia interrupted, eyes flashing with excitement. "I didn't think he was around, it's been so long since he's been spotted." She turned to Tony and gave him a secret smile. "Do you think he knows?"

"Knows what? What have I missed?" *Tía* Consuela

36

took her seat at the opposite end of the table—the chair that their grandmother had always used—after setting down a steaming platter of chicken enchiladas.

Sophia grasped her husband's hand to her chest and waited for his amused nod before looking at her family with a tremulous smile. "We're pregnant," she revealed.

There was a moment of stunned silence, then the room erupted. Consuela cried and jumped to her feet, running around the table to hug the daughter of her heart. Matt and Cass added their congratulations to the mix, and Aaron reached across the table to shake Tony's hand while his sister gushed at him.

"Are you happy for me, brother-of-mine?"

Impossible not to be. Tony and Sophia fairly radiated love and joy of life. It made Aaron's chest ache. His brother and sister were incredibly lucky. They'd both found their happily-ever-after, while he...had let his go.

Trish prodded him with her elbow. Startled, he glanced sideways to see her staring at him with a raised brow. "Well, are you going to say something?"

Why did you leave me? Probably not the time to bring *that* up. Especially with pretty boy sitting next to her with a sardonic grin flirting about his lips.

Aaron turned away from the urge to rearrange his face and circled around to wrap Sophia in his arms, swinging her off her feet. "It's about damn time," he muttered in her ear. "You're going to be an amazing mother."

Astonished laughter turned to tears at his words. She

swiped them away and smacked his arm. "Darn hormones. I hope you're right. We haven't had the easiest of childhoods, have we?"

Aaron caught Matt's eye over her shoulder, his chest warming in a rare familial connection with his taciturn brother. While the death of their parents and grandfather had been tough on all of them, it was Matthew who'd taken it the hardest. He'd been twelve when the plane went down, changing their lives forever—a young boy on the cusp of becoming a man.

"We did all right," he said, thinking of the times Grandma Maddie had comforted three lost and lonely kids when she had to be enduring the depths of despair herself, along with fear for an uncertain future.

"Yeah, we did," she murmured, squeezing his arm before returning to her husband's side. "The baby is due in the spring. Tony and I are over the moon."

Trish's smile was tremulous. "I'm so happy for you. Please, let me know if there's anything you need." She exchanged a long look with her parents, then rose to give a toast. "To the baby."

Everyone echoed her salute and sipped their drinks, but the mood had changed. Aaron sensed the distress Trish tried to cover with forced gaiety and wondered what it meant.

Only one way to find out.

"Trish, would you mind helping me in the kitchen?"

"But—" Consuela began, then a sly grin dimpled her

cheeks. "Yes, yes, thank you, my boy," she said as though no one caught on to the obvious ploy.

Except maybe the boyfriend, who was too busy trying to stay awake to care.

"Umm, sure," Trish said, though her eyes warned him to back off. Too bad he wasn't known for listening. He planned to find out why the mention of babies upset her so much, and he wasn't going to take a none-of-your-business explanation.

TRISH LED the way down the seemingly endless hallway, conscious of the grim man dogging her steps. If only Sophia hadn't... *Stop that.* Of course, Sophia should be thrilled at the promise of a child and wish to share the news with her family. It was an honor to have been included in the revelation. If only she'd been more prepared for the announcement.

"Well," Aaron said, shutting them into the homey kitchen. "Are you going to explain what that was about, or am I supposed to drag it out of you?"

No beating around the bush, then. Trust Aaron to dive in where angels feared to tread. Needing a moment to gather herself, Trish circled the island and made busywork plating up the chocolate cake with a creamy cinnamon frosting Consuela had made earlier in the day. She got a bit of icing on her finger and, without thinking, licked it off, groaning at the delicious taste.

"Your cook is a genius," she said, opening her eyes to find Aaron's intense gaze fixed on her mouth. Her cheeks heated and it wasn't from the spice.

He cleared his throat and shifted his attention to the cake. "Mexican chocolate cake. She usually makes it for special occasions. Do you think...?"

"That she guessed your sister was pregnant?" Trish supplied. She set the knife down and wiped her hands on the wet cloth draped over the sink. "I wouldn't be surprised. Sophia is showing all the obvious signs; emotional, nauseous, glowing. The first three months are a roller-coaster, after that it gets easier—for most women anyway."

Aaron's gaze sharpened. "And what makes *you* a pro on the subject of pregnancies?"

Damn it. She'd known the time would come. Her parents had no idea—this was going to cause all sorts of complications. But Aaron deserved the truth.

"You'd better sit down," she muttered, suddenly in need of a chair herself.

His brows rose and a growing suspicion built like a bank of forbidding clouds in his expressive eyes. "Why do I get a feeling I'm not going to like where this is going?" He hooked a heel around one of the high-backed bar stools and sank onto the swivel seat. "No more games, Trish. I want the truth."

If only it was that easy.

She took the other chair and tried to come up with a way of explaining that wouldn't make her sound like a gold-digger. There was so much more to the story—things that would forever destroy any tender feelings Aaron might have carried for her.

"I know," she said, "because I've been through it." She watched the questions form and hurried to stop him before he could give them voice. "It was a while ago. I was too young, not ready for that kind of responsibility." She gazed unseeingly at the butcher block counter, caught in the agony of past mistakes. "My parents didn't understand how I could be so foolish— careless." A pained laugh escaped. "That's all they were worried about, how it would reflect on them as parents with an unwed, *pregnant* daughter." She shook her head and brushed away angry tears. "I know, it sounds archaic in this day and age, but my family is very traditional. The man is the ruler of the house. I had no choice. They decided to find me a *husband*," she spat the word out, "one that would overlook my *foolish* mistake."

Aaron was silent for so long she finally chanced a look, only to recoil at the anger emanating from his tall frame.

"Are you telling me you had a baby?" He grabbed her wrist and she flinched. "Was it mine, Trish?" Her guilty face gave it away. "Holy hell, it was."

He flung her hand away and rose in a rush to pace the kitchen, ignoring the resulting clatter as the stool hit the floor.

Tears leaked down her cheeks. He was so angry. She

didn't know how they were going to get past this, but for their child's sake they had to find a way.

He stopped, the width of the island between them and scrubbed a hand over a bristly jaw, sending a wanton shiver up her spine. *No, no, no.* Their situation was complicated enough, an unwanted attraction was cruel and unnecessary punishment.

Aaron braced his hands on the countertop, arms rigid with disapproval. "I don't know what to say. Why didn't you tell me?"

My parents threatened your family if I did. Of course, she couldn't tell him that. In fact, anything she said was going to look bad, so she kept quiet.

"Is that your answer to everything? Clam up when times get hard?" He slammed his hand down, shaking the dessert dishes and making her suck in a fearful breath. "This is bullshit."

More tears fell. She owed him an explanation—it hurt immeasurably that she couldn't give him one.

He sighed and handed her a napkin. "Sorry. You caught me off guard. I didn't mean to scare you."

She gratefully accepted the cloth and dabbed at her eyes, chest hurting. "Don't... don't apologize, please. I feel bad enough already."

He reached over the counter and tipped her chin so he could see her face. "Why did you hide it from me, then? We could have worked something out, Trish."

Funny, that was the argument she'd had with her parents. They didn't care.

She leaned away so he'd have to release his hold, his touch a distraction she couldn't afford. "We'd... I'd ended our relationship months before. How would you have reacted if I suddenly arrived on your doorstep pregnant?"

His nostrils flared. "I guess we'll never know." He crossed his arms as though bracing for a blow. "Is the child healthy?"

The depth of emotion in his voice closed her throat. She swallowed hard and nodded. "Perfect. She's beautiful."

He froze. "A girl?"

She nodded, her heart full. "I named her after your grandmother, Madeline Rose."

Now it was his turn to reach for a napkin, his eyes suspiciously moist. "Ah, Trish, you slay me. Thank you for that."

Even in the midst of a betrayal, this man was a better person than all of her family put together. She would never allow her parents to destroy him.

Never.

8

Aaron rode the west side of the property, searching for the fence break his brother had warned him about. He'd been away from the ranch for three days, needing the time to process Trish's shocking announcement.

He was a father.

He barely remembered his own dad. A big, burly man with a hearty laugh, and... the aroma of cinnamon? Yeah, that was it. He'd quit smoking and had taken to chewing on cinnamon-flavored toothpicks to rid himself of the habit. Funny, he'd forgotten that until now.

Madeline Rose.

She'd be what, two now? Walking and talking, laughing and crying. God, he hated Trish for keeping her from him. He'd left her standing in the kitchen the other night before he did something he'd regret—like shaking some sense into her. Truthfully, his head was a mess.

He'd never seen himself as a dad to some cute little munchkin. And she would be cute—look at Trish. But hell, he barely took care of himself, how was he going to handle responsibility for a child? Then again, he couldn't be much worse than the jerk Trish planned to marry. The thought of her in that guy's bed, doing all the things they'd done together, was slowly driving him crazy. Why did she have to come storming into his life just when he'd started to think he was over her?

It wasn't fair.

His lips quirked. How many times had he said those same three words to Grandma Maddie? Too many to count, that's for sure. He'd been convinced his role as middle child was to take all the blame for everything that went wrong in his brother and sister's lives, and he'd resented the hell out of it. Hindsight brought clarity. He could better understand Matthew's apathy now, and Sophia's manic need for attention. They'd been as lost as him—three suddenly rudderless kids. Thank God for Madeline Shaughnessy.

A trail of flattened grass led him to the hole in the fence. Aaron ground-tied Dickens and reached into the saddlebags for his repair kit. He crouched by the break and frowned; the wire had been cut. No horse could create damage like this. He stood and took a slow look at the hills and shadows surrounding the area. Remote. If he was a horse thief, he'd search for a site just like this one. There was even a dirt road between their land and the next ranch that could be used for hauling the animals away. He'd better get hold of the authorities and see what they had to say—right after he told his brother the good news.

He strung fresh wire around the brace post a couple of times and stapled it, then used a wire tool to wrap the excess around the main wire and trimmed the extra with pliers. Next, he went down the line and used a rope fence puller to remove most of the slack. Using a come-along he cranked until the wire was tight before stapling it to the waiting pole, careful not to over-tighten and have the whole thing spring back in his face. He'd seen the damage that caused, it wasn't pretty.

Finished, he wiped his brow and unhooked the canteen from his saddle to take care of his thirst. Only three more to go. Might as well get it over with and place a call to the ranch. He dug out his cell and watched Dickens grazing while waiting for Matthew to pick up on the other end.

"Find the break?" Matt's surly tone carried over the air waves.

Aaron looked at his phone and debated the wisdom of hanging up. Probably not a good idea. Tempting though. "Hello to you, too. Yeah, I'm fine, thanks for asking." He gave up on the sarcasm to convey his worries. "I think the Ghost Stallion might be the least of our problems. Someone slashed the fence."

The silence was deafening. He squinted up at the sun, debating how many hours of daylight he had left to get the job done. He'd be cutting it close.

"Matt, you there?" He tried to control his impatience, really, he did. "Look, if you got nothin' to say, I'm hanging up. I have work to do, as you so generously pointed out the other night."

Matthew breathed a frustrated sigh. "Do you ever get tired of being annoying? I was *trying* to process what you said. I can't remember a time when we ever had to worry about horse thieves—what the hell?"

That was the million-dollar question, wasn't it? The ranching community was a small one; neighbors who looked out for each other. If there were thieves in the area, the locals would band together until the culprits were caught.

"Better get on the phone, bro. The sheriff's department will want to know about this."

"We needed this right now like a hole in the head. How are we going to explain a police presence to our guests?" Papers rustled in Aaron's ear. "Maybe we should return their payments and close down the dude ranch for now. Sophia's going to be disappointed."

Sophia wasn't the only one.

Dickens snorted and shifted restlessly, pulling Aaron's attention to the far-off roar of a diesel engine. The vehicle noise gained in volume, resonating through the hills. His pulse kicked up a notch and he grasped the trailing reins—just in case. "Umm, unless you've already sent the bat signal and the Cavalry is on the way, we have company."

There was a beat of silence and then Matt snapped,

"If you're saying what I think you're saying, get the hell out of there."

Aaron shook his head. Miles away and his brother still tried to boss him around. "Don't get your knickers in a knot. I'm not playing hero. I just want to get a look at whoever it is, see what they're up to." He grabbed the pommel and swung into the saddle, leading Dickens away from the fence and possible exposure. "Don't worry about me. For all we know it's the Smiths out for an afternoon drive."

Steam practically warmed his ear. "You are the most foolhardy, irresponsible..."

"Yada, yada. Hanging up now. Call the sheriff." He tapped the end button and tucked his phone into his back pocket. Matthew meant well, he just had to realize they weren't kids anymore.

A stand of Desert Willow gave him the cover he needed to watch the road without being seen. He waited no more than five minutes before a fancy new tractor-trailer unit rumbled into view, spewing black smoke and dust behind him. Not exactly a vehicle for going incognito. Maybe he was right, and it was locals out doing their thing.

That theory was blown out of the water when the truck slowed as it reached the same section of fence he'd been working to repair. Dickens tossed his head, nose quivering. Aaron patted his neck and murmured to keep him quiet. "Don't go giving us away, pal. We need to find out what they're up to."

Two men, one tall, the other short and stalky, hopped down from the rig and went around back to open the trailer doors. A ramp lowered and a minute later, three horses—Matt's Andalusians if he wasn't mistaken—were unloaded and led up to the single wire holding the fence together. The men looked at each other, shrugged, and used Aaron's tools to cut the line before ushering the animals through. They smacked the last one on the rump and laughed as it bucked and kicked out at them, then nipped at the horse in front to get it moving. They raced up the hill and out of sight while the men watched, cigarettes hanging from their lips.

Aaron swore under his breath. The men wore caps to counter the sun's harsh glare, but it also prevented him from getting a good look. He was tempted to ride out there and ask them what the hell they thought they were doing, but it could get him killed and he wasn't quite ready to die today. Trish and her revelation ran through his mind, convincing him to err on the side of caution. If he could get a photo of the truck and better yet, the license plate, he'd be happy.

The men butted their smokes on the fence post, then headed for the truck. Aaron's hands sweated as he dug his phone out and opened the camera feature. Damn, too far away. He kneed Dickens, guiding him through the undergrowth and closer to the revving black one-ton. The vehicle pulled out and he took his chance, trotting into the open to get a shot of the back bumper. Thankfully, they took no notice of him and drove off. Either they didn't care if they were seen, or they were idiots. A simple search of the plates and the sheriff could arrest their asses.

Unless, the truck was stolen. That was it, had to be. Which meant he was no better off than before. Except they had their stock back—which made no damn sense at all—and they'd left their DNA behind.

He rode over to the fence pole, dismounted, and using his work gloves, collected the discarded cigarette butts and placed them in a side pocket of his saddlebag. Look at him, going all P.I., now if it only helped to catch the culprits.

9

Trish sat in the den, mindlessly skimming through a journal on horse husbandry while waiting for the moment Aaron came home, though she tried to tell herself otherwise. It had been days without word. She was beginning to believe he planned to stay away until their family left. Not that she could blame him. When she thought of the expression on his face when she'd told him about Madeline... sucker-punched. That's the only way to describe it. She was probably lucky he hadn't thrown them all out. Father would love that.

Then she heard him. She didn't even need to see him to know he'd arrived. The deep rumble of his voice as he spoke to someone in the entry foyer sent delicious shivers up her spine. "Stop it," she muttered. This dangerous attraction had to end. She was engaged, for Pete's sake.

Besides, he hated her now.

She set the tome aside, and rose, hands nervously fluttering over the magenta silk of her dress—as though she'd known he'd be back today. Would he search her out, or should she go to him? Would he even *want* to see her again? Now the truth was out, she felt an overwhelming sense of relief. She'd hated keeping his daughter from him, if only... It didn't matter anymore. Her parents, and Kyle, were going to have to accept Aaron's place in their lives. It was done.

The doorbell rang and curiosity drove her to the hallway. She peeked out and was surprised to see a lawman, notepad in hand, talking to Aaron and his brother, Matthew. All three men wore identical grim expressions—Trish's heart fluttered, as though facing an unseen threat. She must have made an involuntary sound because the stranger glanced her way, then straightened. He removed his hat as he stepped forward, brushing past Aaron and Matthew.

"And who is this vision of loveliness you've been hiding away?" he teased, moving to take her hand in a surprisingly firm shake.

Her father used to tell her you could tell the quality of a man from his handshake. Judging by the sheriff's— she could read the label on his badge this close up—he was strong and capable. Hopefully, she was wrong in this case because something told her trouble had just come calling.

Aaron had followed and performed the introductions, though she could tell he wasn't happy. "Trish

Sylvester and her family are our first visitors since we opened the guest ranch."

The officer released his grip, but his calm eyes remained watchful. "I bet you didn't expect horse thieves as part of the package."

Trish startled, glancing between Matthew and Aaron. "Horse thieves? Did someone steal your horses? Why would anyone want to do that?"

Aaron chuckled. "Oh, that's not the craziest part. They returned them a few days later."

"I fail to see the humor." Matt glared at his brother. "This is serious."

The smile disappeared from Aaron's lips. His shoulders tensed. "You know, you can be a real asshat sometimes."

"Cut it out you two, you're in mixed company," the sheriff said mildly. His attention remained fixed on Trish, and she had to force herself not to squirm under his regard. "You look familiar, miss. Have you been in these parts before?"

His good-ol' boy Texan charm didn't fool her for an instant. The sheriff was on a fishing expedition, she just had to figure out why and what he wanted from her. "It was a while ago, but yes. I live in Austin, though."

"Austin, the city that never sleeps. For some reason, I didn't figure you for a city slicker."

Aaron coughed what sounded suspiciously like *bull* into his hand. "You blind, man? Look at that dress? It has dinner and a theatre written all over it. Leave the girl alone, Stan. She has nothing to do with it."

The sheriff's brow lifted, but he backed up a step or two, giving Aaron room to place his intimidating body between them. Trish hadn't been bothered by Stan. She couldn't say the same about the aggravating man who'd decided she needed protection. If the sheriff didn't have her on his list of suspects before, he would now. *Damn it, Aaron.*

She needed to talk to her father. "If you'll excuse me, it's been a long day. I think I'll take a nap before dinner."

It was Matthew who answered, his gaze distrustful. "We'll expect you at six, then," he said, a warning implicit in the words. Be there, or else...

She gave the sheriff a nervous smile and touched Aaron's stiff back. "See you later?"

He met her gaze over his shoulder and a spark of awareness jumped between them. "Count on it."

Trish turned and walked sedately down the hall toward her parents' room, all the while fighting the instinct to flee. She didn't know what she'd do if her fears came to fruition. Her father could be a vindictive man and when Matthew and Aaron had backed out of a multi-million-dollar deal with their company, she'd been afraid it would only be a matter of time before he sought retribution.

But this... it made no sense. Why steal a horse, only to return it at a later date?

She knocked on the solid wood paneling of the door,

absently noting the mahogany chair rail lining the wall, a match to the door and beautiful terracotta tile flooring. This home radiated love and attention to detail—a far cry from the austere blandness of her parents' house.

Her mother opened the door, narrow face pinched. "Your father is resting."

Read, *go away.*

They put on a convincing act in public, but the truth was, Trish felt like a square bolt in the round hole of her family dynamics—she didn't fit. Her older brother was the favored child, voted most likely to succeed. Ever since she could remember, Father had groomed Andy to step into his shoes, the heir apparent. It didn't matter that Trish was a natural in the numbers game, she was a woman. Women did *not* run the Sylvester Corporation.

"I need to see him," she said now, determined to confront him and get to the bottom of this mess.

"Patricia, not..."

"Let her in," her father grumbled. "I'm awake after all your nattering anyway."

Her mother reluctantly permitted her entry into the room and Trish shot her a triumphant glance. She'd beaten the gatekeeper—go her.

Her father lay flat on his back, hands folded over his chest, covers barely wrinkled. Trish wasn't sure if she was reassured by that, or not. Obviously, he wasn't wrestling with a guilty conscience.

"Daddy, we need to talk." She cringed on the inside. What was with the revision to childhood all of a sudden?

He huffed out a sigh and sat up, waving her to a nearby chair in olive green. His robe gaped, showing a bony chest and protruding Adam's apple. He yanked the material closed and tightened his belt. "Well, get on with it then. What has you all flustered? That Shaughnessy boy back already?"

Already? Aaron had been gone for three days, and she was pretty sure it was her fault.

"Yes, he's here. After all, it *is* his home." She rose from the chair to pace the room, avoiding the corner where her mother sat pretending to read a newspaper. "The police are here, also. Seems someone decided to steal livestock and then return the animals like damaged merchandise." Trish turned in time to catch her father's speculative expression. Her stomach sank. "Please tell me you didn't have anything to do with this."

The newspaper rattled as her mother threw it down. "How dare you accuse your father of theft. Apologize right now, young lady." Even angry, not a stray hair fell out of place. It was amazing, really.

"Never mind that," Father said. "Was Shaughnessy upset?"

Seriously? That's what he had to say? Trish felt like smacking a palm to her forehead. Or maybe his.

"Where are Kyle and Andy, Dad? I thought Kyle was picking him up from the airport." She took her seat again and stared her father in the eye. "Did Kyle steal those horses for you?"

Something that looked suspiciously like satisfaction

passed over his expression before he wiped it clean. "Is that what you think of your *fiancé*? Of me? I thought I raised you better."

If by raising her better he meant teaching her never to trust a shark, yeah, he'd done a good job at that. "If you've broken the law, I'm not going to be able to get you out of it this time, and I think you know why."

Her mother sniffed from her corner, but her father... he just nodded. "You have nothing to worry your pretty little head about." Then he rose and entered the bathroom, closing the door with a decisive snap.

If only her pretty little head believed him.

10

Aaron was relaxing in the courtyard with a cold beer when Sophia joined him by the fountain. He eyed her arrival with a touch of cynicism, certain Matthew had sent her to talk to him.

Sure enough, she opened with his big adventure. "So, I hear you were playing hero today. That wasn't very smart." She looked as though she'd like to clip him behind the ear if she wasn't so short.

His lips quirked. "I forgot my cape at home, or I might have managed more than a snapshot."

She smacked his arm instead. "Not funny, wise guy. What if those hoodlums stopped the truck? Did you have a plan 'B'? Of course not," she rambled, on a roll now. "You always had a dangerous urge to prove yourself. Remember when you hopped onto that Brahma bull Matthew brought in for breeding purposes? He was fit to be tied. You're damn lucky you didn't get killed."

"By him or the bull? And. ow." Aaron rubbed his arm, which actually did sting. His sister was not a dainty little gal—unlike a certain someone who he was most definitely *not* going to think about tonight. N.O.T., *No On Trish.*

"Take your punishment like a man," Sophia said, sitting on the narrow fountain ledge so she could trail her fingers in the cool water. As kids, they'd often played in the water on warm summer evenings, diving after the coins at the bottom as though they were treasure hunters. Aaron privately thought his parents tossed the money in just to keep them occupied. Whoever it was, they had enjoyed the bounty. His chest warmed at the memory. It was rare for him to remember anything before the plane crash, and after, well... nothing was the same.

"At least you're acknowledging I'm a man, it's a step in the right direction," he teased, rubbing his sister's curly head.

Sophia ducked away. "Cut it out. You know I hate it when you do that." She lifted her hands to straighten her hair and her arched back highlighted a slight baby bump.

A different set of emotions swamped him now; ones of pride and love in equal measure. His baby sister was having a child. He vowed then and there to guard it like his... own. And there he was—back to Trish. The mere thought of her skeevy boyfriend/fiancé stepping in as Aaron's daughter's hero chaffed his nerves in ways he couldn't explain. And the worst of it was there wasn't a damn thing he could do about it.

"What's that surly glare for? I'm the one getting assaulted." Sophia peered at him through the intensity of the late afternoon sun, the rays turning the courtyard golden.

"I'm not glaring," he denied. "I'm wondering why you're out here with me instead of cuddling with your one true love." He was happy for Sophia and Tony, their road to wedded bliss hadn't been an easy one. But he couldn't deny an underlying envy at the same time. If not for Trish's disappearing act last spring, this could have been them. He'd tried more than once to reach her so they could talk out whatever had gone wrong but was cut off at every turn. Rather than beating his head against a wall that was never coming down, he'd given up. But in the deepest, darkest nights, he wondered if he shouldn't have tried harder.

"What, I'm not allowed to spend time with my favorite brother? Don't tell Matthew," she added, grinning.

Little minx. She'd made a game out of pitting brother against brother most of their childhoods. She loved them equally, he knew that, she just had to stir the pot. "He wouldn't believe me if I did," he muttered, taking another pull from his beer. The words came out by rote, he'd said them in a variety of ways most of his life. It wasn't that he wanted to be his big brother, hell no, responsibility wasn't his thing, but a little respect now and then wouldn't hurt. Or then again, knowing Matt, maybe it would.

"You're too hard on yourself," Sophia said, rising to

circle the fountain. "So... was it scary chasing down those horse thieves?" The sparkle in her eyes changed scary to exciting.

She'd always been the wild child, impossible to control—at least until their grandmother died. She'd changed then, they all had.

"I wish I could have caught them," he admitted. "But I know my limits. Hopefully the sheriff can use the photos I took to get a positive ID on the truck and trailer unit. Something tells me they're local, otherwise how did they know about that old road? I barely remembered it was there."

Sophia held up her cellphone. "If you have one of these, it's relatively easy to find anything nowadays." She came back to his side and rested a hand on his arm. "Let the police do their job, Aaron. I only have two brothers, I'd like to keep them around for a while."

The disquiet in her expression stopped him from brushing off her concern. She was pregnant now, the last thing she needed was to be worrying about her dumbass siblings. On the other hand, it was their job to make sure the ranch was safe for everyone.

"I'll make you a deal," he said. "I'll stay out of the sheriff's way—for now—if you tell me why in the world you thought it was a good idea to invite the Sylvesters to the ranch? You had to know it was only going to cause problems."

She stared up at him, a confusing jumble of emotions flitting across her expressive features. "I .. I..."

"It's okay, Sophia," came a sultry voice that played havoc with his dreams. He turned and met Trish's defiant gaze. "It's my fault."

TRISH BIT down on her bottom lip, nerves getting the best of her. As Aaron leaned protectively over his sister, all she could think was how much she wished he'd do the same for her. And how messed up was that? She had a fiancé. They were supposed to get married just a few short months from now. And yet... there were all these *feelings* swarming around her chest like a pack of angry wasps when it came to the man staring back at her with enigmatic eyes.

And now he was going to want answers she wasn't ready to give.

"Sophia agreed to our coming under duress," she said, crossing her arms in defence.

Sophia gave a braying little laugh that carried across the courtyard. "It wasn't as bad as all that," she assured her brother. "I'd set up a website for the dude ranch a few days earlier but hadn't opened it to reservations. Trish called to say how beautiful it looked and when we were launching, and the rest, as they say, is history."

"I can't believe Trish was that interested in our affairs. It never mattered to her before."

A stagnant silence fell after Aaron's bitter outburst. Sophia sent her a helpless glance before hugging her brother's stiff frame. "I'd better head inside and see if Consuela needs help with dinner. Coming?"

Aaron's gaze remained fixed on Trish, causing a parade of goosebumps to march along her spine. "In a bit. I want to finish my beer first."

Sophia gave a reluctant nod and squeezed Trish's hand on her way by—and then it was just the two of them. Funny how she could handle a hundred corporate tycoons, but one lanky, attitude-ridden cowboy filled her with trepidation. Her mouth felt like it was filled with cotton balls and her heart beat painfully against her ribs, while Aaron stood there cool as a cucumber. It was beyond annoying.

"Can we talk about this or are you going to continue to be a jackass?" She faced off with him, hands on hips. He wasn't the only one with a bone to pick.

He tipped his bottle to her before taking a long drink, the movement pulling his western shirt tight over broad shoulders. Suddenly it was her turn to be thirsty, but not for beer.

Grimacing, she waited him out, determined to get their ugly feelings out in the open so they could move on —for their daughter's sake.

Finally, he set the bottle on the edge of the fountain and gestured for her to take a seat. "Come on, I'm not going to bite. I'd rather the entire family didn't know my business." He went brows up toward the windows of the hacienda, open to take in the unseasonably warm afternoon air.

Trish didn't have much experience with nosy family members. Her brother, Andy, was ten years older than she was and hadn't been around much during her formative years, and her parents... well, the less said about them the better.

She settled on the wide rim of the fountain, careful to keep a demure distance from the foot he'd raised to rest next to his beer. If her parents, or Kyle, were to glance outside she didn't want them thinking this was an assignation. Things were more than complicated enough.

"Where is... the child?" Aaron asked, his tone abrupt.

Her spine stiffened. "She's staying with a close friend. Don't worry, she has three kids of her own, Madeline is perfectly safe. Besides, I've been calling every day since we left." She smiled, thinking of Maddie's soft babbling. "She's having a blast. Sarah's kids spoil her rotten."

"Can I see a picture?" Aaron's walnut-brown eyes had warmed as she spoke, sending a shiver of awareness to flutter in her belly.

"Of course, I should have thought of it sooner." She fumbled getting her phone out of her pocket and took a deep breath. *Get a grip.* Yes, he was a handsome man. Yes, his smile was like a ray of sunshine after a long winter's storm, but he didn't belong to her. She'd given up that right. Not that she'd had a choice.

She opened the folder set aside just for Madeline. Her daughter in all her cherubic sweetness smiled out at them in varying stages of growth.

"She's an itty-bitty little thing," Aaron murmured, his forefinger tracing the bundle in the pink hospital blanket Trish held with such care.

"I had... trouble with my pregnancy and she came earlier than expected." Trish's stomach clenched remembering *why* she'd had issues with the birth. "The doctor kept Madeline in an incubator for a couple of months to allow her more time to develop. She's fine though," she hurried to add.

"She's perfect," Aaron agreed, his voice a couple of octaves lower than normal. He lifted his gaze to mesh with hers and Trish's heart skipped a beat. "She has your eyes, they're beautiful." His mouth hovered a breath away and then it was there, touching hers, and the world slipped away.

He'd cast a spell over her.

It had always been this way between the two of them; an instant, undeniable connection unlike anything she'd felt since. Even as she lifted her lips to his, desperate to hold onto the moment, the man, for as long as possible, the futility of their attraction washed over her.

As though sensing her disquiet, he lifted his head, eyes dark and hooded. "Come away with me," he said, and for a too-brief moment her heart soared. "I need you."

For how long? If he found out the truth, he would hate her family. Hate her. She'd sooner live the lie.

She extracted herself from his arms and stood, shivering without his touch. "It's too late, Aaron. I... love Kyle. Please don't kiss me like that again." *I can't take it.*

Shadows chased across his expression before he donned the cynical, jaded look he'd managed to perfect. "Sure, darlin', whatever you say. Can't blame a guy for trying." He picked up his discarded beer and sauntered into the hacienda without a backward glance while tears streamed down Trish's cheeks.

11

Plans for the upcoming Harvest Ball moved along at a steady pace, with Sophia in her element. Aaron did his best to stay out of the way, but his sister knew all his hideouts and eventually tracked him down in the horse barn.

"There you are, I was beginning to think you were avoiding me," she said, entering Dickens' stall. "I need help."

Aaron finished filing his horse's back hoof before patting the smooth flank. He looked at Sophia over the broad back. "I knew it couldn't last," he sighed. "Okay, what do you need?"

She huffed out an exasperated breath. "Don't sound so excited. I'm doing this for the ranch, you know."

He did know. Unfortunately, it didn't make having their home overrun by strangers any more palatable. In all fairness, Sophia had gone over and above on the website and the hacienda. He was no tech guru but even he would pay the astronomical prices to stay as their guest. Her sales pitch was nothing short of genius.

But she looked tired.

If only the agricultural firm he'd shown his ideas to would call back with a contract—none of this would be necessary. He ducked under Dickens' neck and came up next to his sister. "Shouldn't you be taking it easy?"

She patted her growing baby bump and smiled. "You sound like Tony. I'm fine. It's just there's a hundred and one things to get done and only a few days left before the big event. This ball will give us the free advertising we need to get the guest ranch off the ground. I've invited some of my old contacts from New York and Trish promised to put the word out, too. She's been great, Aaron. I would have been lost without her."

The mention of Trish sent the now familiar fluttery feeling to his stomach. He'd spent the last couple of days rehashing that kiss by the fountain; the near-desperation in his voice when he'd begged her to come away with him. Her negative reaction.

He was an idiot to keep bashing his heart against the stone wall of Trish's soul. She'd made it clear when she left him the first time that he wasn't enough. Why would anything be different now?

"I'm happy for you, Sis, really I am. I just wish..." He brushed a curly lock of hair behind her ear.

She grabbed his hand and held on, her eyes giant pools in a pale face. "I know this isn't what you and

Matthew wanted for the ranch. But it *is* my dream. Can't you give it a chance? Please?"

Sophia asked so little of him. Surely, he could get his head out of his ass long enough to give her this one small thing. Besides, the ranch needed the aid.

He smiled and chucked her under the chin. "Okay, you win. I'm at your command. What do you need me to do?"

Now that she was getting her way, her shoulders relaxed. "It's the barn. I plan to hold the harvest dance there Saturday night, but it needs serious help. I should have checked first. I just assumed it was in good shape. The floor is rotting, there's a hole in the roof, and the entire place smells like... like, manure." Her nose crinkled up adorably.

Aaron laughed outright at that. "You do realize this is a working horse and cattle ranch, right?"

Sophia slapped his arm. "Not funny. Ever since I became pregnant with this one," she glanced down at her belly, "I seem to have developed an aversion to certain... scents. Sorry, Dickens." She held out the apple she'd pulled from her pocket. Dickens snuffled her palm before gently plucking the fruit from her hand and crunching it down with his blunt yellow teeth. "So, do you think you can get it done in time for the dance?"

Three days. Nothing like an impossible task to get his mind off his troubles. "I'll do my best—no promises," he warned.

She threw her arms around him anyway. "I owe you

one," she whispered before heading for the stall door. "By the way," she said from outside the stall, "Trish is going to help with the decorating so don't be surprised if you see her there."

DESPITE HER MISGIVINGS, Trish arrived at the aged wooden barn on the edge of the Shaughnessy compound early the next morning. She still couldn't believe she'd allowed Sophia to talk her into working with Aaron. She shuddered to think how he felt about the whole thing. And if that wasn't bad enough, she'd omitted telling Kyle and her parents what she was up to.

The old gray barn hunched on top of a slight hill, tall Bigtooth maples guarding the entrance. There was a worn dirt path winding its way to the wide double doors standing open to accept the morning sun. Trish could easily envision crushed white rock covering the path and hundreds of fairy lights twinkling in the tree branches. Sophia suggested painting the structure white, but Trish liked the aged beauty of the old building. Giant vases filled with sunflowers, chrysanthemums and goldenrod along with strings of Edison bulbs would go a long way to softening the barn's forbidding visage. Maybe a few strategically placed bales of hay, pumpkins and gourds...

"You planning on standing there all day?"

Trish's gaze jumped to the jean-clad cowboy leaning against the doorframe, hat tipped over his forehead to block the light. No one wore a pair of blue jeans like Aaron Shaughnessy. Long, muscular legs, worn cowboy boots, the swagger, all of it called to her on a purely molecular level. He was her every fantasy wrapped in an annoying male package.

Sighing, she climbed the slope to his side. "Good morning to you, too. Is that for me?" she asked, reaching for the travel mug in his hand.

He gave it over without argument, causing her to sniff the opening before hazarding a drink. Coffee. Strong, black, manna from heaven. Okay, maybe this wouldn't be so bad after all.

"I don't know why Sophia decided to put the two of us together on this project, it wasn't my idea." Aaron eyed the tablet in her hands and raised a sandy brow. "Mind telling me what that thing is for?"

On second thought—Trish ignored him to glance into the cavernous space behind them. "So, this is the dance hall? It doesn't look so bad."

He gave her an incredulous look. "You're kidding, right? There are holes in the roof and the floor is rotten. Hell, a stiff wind would blow the whole thing over."

She didn't believe Sophia would have chosen this venue if it was as bad as Mr. Dramatic wanted her to think. Sure, there were a few issues—even she could see that—but if he quit complaining and tried to put a positive foot forward, they could get it done. They had to, Sophia was counting on them and after everything Trish's family had done to theirs, she was determined to get this one thing right. With or without Aaron Shaughnessy.

"Were you born this happy or did you have to work at it?" Trish asked under her breath. "Look," she said louder, "I'm sure if we exert some effort, we can make this barn shine, and help your sister who is doing way too much for a pregnant lady. It's only three days, come on, what do you say?"

Maybe it was selfish, but somewhere in the midst of her spiel, she'd come to the realization that she wanted time with him. After this weekend, they would only see each other every other holiday when Aaron took Madeline—that is if he agreed to shared custody, they hadn't even gotten around to talking about that yet—while she sat at home wishing things could have been different.

Her heart needed this chance to heal.

"I can spare a couple of guys; we'll start on the roof today and tackle that floor tomorrow. I hope you're ready to pull some long hours, it's going to be tight." He reclaimed his coffee and took a drink, his breath fogging in the crisp morning air. "What are you thinking?"

That you aren't the tough guy you want people to believe you are. Outwardly, she smiled. "I'm thinking we need more coffee." Before she gave into the urge to rest her head on his shoulder and enjoy the sunrise together, she strode into the barn and began to share her ideas to the four walls—they were probably the only ones listening.

12

Aron stopped to wipe sweat off his brow and survey the surrounding countryside from the roof of the old barn. The promise of this morning's sunrise had carried into the afternoon with above normal temperatures, though the trees were showing their fall colors like elegant women at a tea party. It wouldn't be long now until winter cradled the hill country in her chilly hands.

The agricultural corporation had finally gotten back to him. They were going to take his proposal under consideration and let him know their final assessment before spring. So, it wasn't a no, but it was far from a yes, too. A bit early to celebrate, though he'd been tempted to break into the booze after their call. He'd never been a patient man and this indecision was driving him crazy. He knew his idea was a sound solution to the droughts created by climate change, but without their financial backing he didn't see how he was going to get it off the ground. He'd come close last year with Trish's brother, Andy—his funding in exchange for a piece of Balmoral. Except Matt wouldn't sign off on it and the deal had fallen through. That and his non-relationship with Trish Sylvester.

His gaze moved to the shadowy recesses of the barn. Now that the floors had been refinished, Trish had Rico up a ladder hanging strings of lights from beam to beam while another man unloaded square hay bales from a trailer parked outside the doors. She had him setting them up in a haphazard arrangement that gave the large room an open, boho design. Paired with comfortable seating areas draped with Mexican blankets, throw pillows in a wide array of materials and colors, farmhouse side tables painted in shades of white, blue, and yellow, and the candles—hundreds of candles in varying containers and sizes, the whole thing should have looked like a train wreck, but he had to admit he liked it. She laughed at something Rico said, her face turned up to him in amusement. Were they here to flirt or get some work done? Rico must have sensed his razor-eyed glare. He glanced at the roof, caught Aaron's scowl and refocused on the task at hand.

Aaron flung the last board into place and pounded the nails into the wood before gathering his tools and heading for the ladder. If Trish wanted a distraction, he'd give her one, by damn.

He strode to the barn doors and called, "I need to ride out to Hidden Valley, you coming?"

The cheerful smile disappeared, but she nodded. After a quiet word to Rico, who kept his thoughts to himself, *smart man,* she joined him at the entrance. "What do you think? It's coming along better than I expected. Hopefully, your sister will like it."

He'd never thought of Trish as insecure, but her fingers were white where they gripped the tablet she always seemed to carry, almost like a security blanket, and she refused to look him in the eye, her gaze flitting anywhere but his face. His jealousy evaporated under an overwhelming need to reassure this woman who'd once meant the world to him. The mother of his child.

He gently pried the computer from her hands and set it on a nearby hay bale before taking her shoulders and spinning her to face the room, her back to his front having a predictable effect on his body. "Look, Trish. Really look. You've taken a beaten down old behemoth of a building and turned it into a sanctuary. Sophia is going to love it, trust me."

She twisted in his grasp, her beautiful green eyes glowing. "Really? I wasn't sure if it would all meld together like it had in my head—always a scary place." She laughed and he found himself grinning for no good reason. *God, you're beautiful.*

He reluctantly loosened his arms and took a step back. "We'd better get going if we want to return in time for the dance." He'd thought long and hard and had come to the decision that he wanted his daughter in his life. Even if Trish was married to another guy, it didn't mean they couldn't work out an arrangement that would suit everyone. He'd never figured himself for a satellite father, but there it was.

"Are you sure we can't do this later? I'd like to be around if Sophia needs me." Back to the nervous non-stare. What was she up to?

"It's only an hour's ride. Come on, city girl, you can handle it."

Left with no choice, she led the way out of the barn, stopping in surprise when she noticed Dickens and a bay mare standing under the maple tree. She flicked him an ironic glance. "That sure of me, were you?"

Maybe once, not anymore. "I ordered an extra horse saddled on the off-chance," he said, unwilling to argue. "Don't worry, Nelly is a sweetheart."

"It's not the horse that concerns me," she muttered, reaching for the saddle horn.

She should have looked comical in her stylish jeans and thigh-length white men's dress shirt—sleeves rolled up and buttons from throat to cleavage undone—instead his pulse stuttered, his hands as sweaty as if he were a gangly teen on his first date. She stumbled, long, *long* leg extended while the other sneaker-clad foot tried to catch up to the stirrup. Aaron caught her around the waist before she fell and hoisted her into the saddle, his fingers lingering until she met his gaze. "You look good on the back of a horse," he said and meant every word. Her posture was straight, hands gentle on the reins. Long blond hair swirled around her shoulders and her skin had taken on a peachy glow he'd like to think was at least partially caused by his touch.

"Thanks," she murmured. "Though I think you're just being kind."

Nope. He wasn't feeling *kind* at the moment. Hot and bothered, yes. Frustrated, hell, yeah. Confused about his feelings, definitely.

He made sure her stirrups were the right length before mounting Dickens. "Ready?"

"As I'll ever be." She gripped the reins and clucked at her horse. "Okay, Nelly, giddy-up."

Aaron kept his smile in check and led out, heading west across the ten-acre pasture that connected Hidden Valley to the main homestead. The breeze played with the last hay crop of the season, creating a golden sea of motion.

Trish rode up beside him. "This is stunning, Aaron. So different from the suburban landscape I'm used to—your family is lucky."

Yeah, he guessed she was right. For him the ranch was home. It was refreshing to see it through her eyes. "It's been Shaughnessy land for over a century. Hard for most folks to imagine these days."

Her smile was tinged with melancholy. "I don't think I've lived in one place for longer than five years. My parents are wanderers."

Aaron thought of his young daughter, Madeline.

That wasn't the life he wanted for her—or for Trish. "Maybe, now that you're getting married," the word soured on his tongue, "you can change that. Start a new tradition."

"I'd like that," she replied. Then added so softly he barely heard her, "If only things were different."

What was he supposed to make from that? Was she sorry for walking away from him? He stiffened. Was her fiancé abusive?

He nudged Dickens closer to Nelly so he could make a grab for the reins, drawing both horses to a dust-churning standstill.

"What are you doing?" Trish cried, her expression startled.

Aaron tipped his hat back and stared her down. "Care to explain what you meant with that statement a moment ago?" If Lane was hurting her, he'd pay—so help him God.

"You're crazy, you know that?" She swatted his hands and retrieved her horse's reins. "You could have gotten us killed."

Unexpectedly, he laughed. "Killed, huh? I'm surprised you agreed to come out with me, then."

She huffed out a sigh, then grinned. "A little over the top, maybe?"

Her hair rivaled the sun for beauty. Aaron ached to bury his hand in those golden threads and kiss her until she admitted they should be together. The old chemistry was there, he could see the same awareness in her eyes that he was feeling. This was ridiculous. Why was she marrying a guy she didn't even love?

"Aaron? You're staring." She fidgeted with those damn three buttons he'd been fantasizing about all day.

He jerked his head to the hills behind him. "The valley is over there. Let's table our differences until then, okay?"

She hesitated and glanced back towards the safety of the ranch—smart girl—before nodding. "I'll go with you, but only because we need to decide what to do about Maddie. I don't want this to turn into an argument though, agreed?"

Hell, no. He wasn't agreeing to anything right now. He didn't trust the Sylvester clan as far as he could throw them, and that included Trish. Which made this attraction damn painful to bear.

13

Sophia sat in front of her desktop computer and sighed. So much to do, so little time, and if that wasn't bad enough, little Egbert here—she patted her slight baby bump—wasn't the politest of guests. Her hormones were running wild with morning sickness, morphing into afternoon sleepiness and evening weep-fests. Poor Tony. He tried so hard to keep her happy, but this baby thing was as new to him as it was to her and she had to wonder if he regretted it. Annnnnd, cue the tears. She loved her baby, they both did. It's just with the pressure of opening the guest house, maybe this wasn't the best time to be pregnant. Understatement of the year.

She kept the books. She knew how bad off the ranch was; how close they were to losing everything. Her family needed her to succeed. She wiped her wet cheeks with trembling fingers before clicking the mouse to the Balmoral Guest Ranch website. Thanks to her history in advertising she'd managed to make a professional-looking, welcoming site, and with the pictures they would add from this weekend's Harvest Dance, the reservations should roll in.

She hoped.

Maybe it had been a mistake to invite Trish and her family to the opening. The Sylvesters were big fish in the investment corporation field, and though Matthew had turned down their offer to buy a portion of the ranch, Trish had approached her with a plan to invest in the venture. And if Sophia could manage to throw Trish and her pig-headed brother, Aaron, together often enough, maybe they would see they were meant for each other.

She prayed.

More than anything, she wanted to see her brothers happy. After their parents died, the boys made a pact to protect her, and she planned to return the favor. If only these *stupid* tears would quit falling so she could get some work done. She was just reaching for a tissue when Matthew strolled into the office, Pippa on his hip.

"Oh, ho," he said, brows peaking. "Aunty has a boo-boo." He hugged his daughter before setting her in the corner with her toys. He made sure Pippa was settled, giving Sophia the time she needed to regain her composure, then sat on one of two leather-tufted chairs across from her desk. "Hormones, or is there something else I need to know about?"

That was Matt. He faced his problems head-on. And family issues were a part of the package. She gave him a wobbly smile and rose to get her aunty hugs from Pippa. "How's Aunty's girl? Are you being good for Daddy?" Pippa was about the cutest child she'd ever seen. Big blue eyes and soft blond curls combined with a light dusting of freckles across the nose and one deep dimple in her right cheek when she giggled. Oh, and that girl's giggles; if Sophia could find a way to bottle them up, the world would be a brighter place.

"She's always good for Daddy, aren't you Pumpkin?" Matthew grinned and Pippa grinned back, revealing that angel's kiss dimple.

She placed a slightly sticky, pudgy palm on Sophia's cheek and stared deep into her eyes. "Daddy says I gets a pet if I'm good. I'm good, right Aunty?"

The little minx stopped just short of a conspiratorial wink. She definitely knew the power she held over the Shaughnessy adults.

Sophia planted a kiss on her cherubic nose. "If Daddy doesn't get you a pet, you come and see me and I'll talk to him, but only if you do as he says. Deal?" She waited for the munchkin's solemn nod before setting her back amongst her toys.

"She's been after Cassandra and me for a pet even though we already have Chewy and Pumpkin in the house. It's hard enough keeping those two under control," Matt said as Sophia moved to her chair.

It was true, Matt's little hairless chihuahua ruled the household and hadn't appreciated Sophia's cat, Pumpkin, when they moved home, at all. But surely there was room for one more. She decided to table the conversation for now and revisit it closer to Pippa's birthday when he might be feeling more generous.

"What brings you into work, isn't it your day off?" She surreptitiously moved her mouse to place her computer to sleep.

"Yes, but no changing the subject. Why were you crying when we arrived?" He crossed his arms and gave her that don't-feed-me-no-bull look he'd perfected as a young teen forced to grow up too fast.

Sophia toyed with using her pregnancy as an excuse, but she'd turned to him for advice so many times over the years, the truth came out instead. "I'm scared I've failed you. The reservations aren't coming in like I expected. Aaron's angry because I invited Trish and her family, and I feel horrible that I've let you down," she said, reaching for a fresh tissue.

Matt uncurled his arms and leaned forward, the intensity in his gaze stopping her tears in their tracks. "You could never disappoint me." He reached across and clasped her hand. "Sophia Mackenzie Morrison, you have Shaughnessy blood and fire flowing through your veins. We don't quit." He gave her fingers a squeeze before letting them go. "We've been through plenty of hard times, and I'm sure there'll be more, but it doesn't matter—do you know why?"

She looked at Pippa playing in the corner, as she'd done herself as a child, at the hundred-year-old map on the wall depicting the ranch and its boundaries, the photo of Matt's prize Andalusian stallion, and the painting Grandma Maddie had commissioned of their parents before the accident. The ties that bind.

"Because we are fam-i-ly," she sang, then sent him a watery smile. "You're a pretty terrific big brother, do you know that?"

He shrugged and grimaced. "I'm also deaf after your singing." He laughed when she threw an eraser at him. Pippa ran over to see what the commotion was about, and her dad swung her into the air and swooped like an airplane. She shrieked with joy and grabbed his hair. He lowered her down and did a raspberry on her belly, reducing her to fits of giggles.

Best. Sound. Ever.

Sophia met his amused gaze over Pippa's tousled head and smiled. They were going to be just fine.

14

Trish followed Aaron through a narrow canyon, the red rock walls close enough to touch, and marveled at the vista opening out before them. A faint game trail led down to a verdant valley filled with lush grass, wildflowers, and even a gentle stream. No wonder the Shaughnessys kept this place a secret.

"It's stunning," she said in all sincerity. Though it paled in comparison to the proud cowboy sitting his horse a few steps ahead of her, the late afternoon sun glinting like gold in his hair.

He glanced back and smiled. A real smile. It stole her breath. "Growing up, this was our playground," he said, waving an arm to encompass the valley. "Whenever we got on Mom's nerves—which was often," he grinned, "Dad would bring us out here to blow off steam. We even stayed in the cabin a few times."

Now that he mentioned it, she could see the dark

brown roof of a log shack nestled under a giant cotton-wood, the leaves a bright yellow gold. "It's breathtaking." And so different from the concrete jungle she'd grown up in.

"Come on." He clucked to his horse and the animal began to make its sure-footed way down the steep grade.

Trish's horse followed suit, not giving her time to get scared. She grasped the pommel with both hands, glued her gaze to Aaron's broad back, and prayed. It was like going downhill on a roller coaster, but without seatbelts and a good deal slower—thank goodness. Pebbles rolled beneath the horses' hooves, sending little puffs of dust floating into the air like signal beacons. Aaron controlled his mount with the slightest of hand movements, glancing back now and again to make sure she hadn't fallen off, she guessed. No chance of that; he was going to have to pry her fingers loose when they got to the bottom.

Then they reached the valley, and she was struck by the peaceful setting. Birds flitted here and there, lark sparrows and Golden-cheeked Warblers, while a Scissor-tailed Flycatcher perched on a fallen log watching them with inquisitive eyes. Bees buzzed, gathering the last of the year's nectar, and a busy squirrel dashed across the trail, cheeks full of his fall harvest. Everywhere she looked, there was movement, and yet she felt a deep calmness settle over her—as though this was a place out of time; a healing ground.

"Stupid really," she murmured, "but I feel as though I've been here before. Maybe in my dreams?" She smiled to lighten the moment. "Was the cabin here when your family bought the land?"

Aaron dismounted at the foot of the steps before answering. He folded his arms over the saddle to stare up at her from under the rim of his cowboy hat. "Nah. My great-granddad built it and brought his bride here until he could build her the hacienda."

Trish looked at the ramshackle shack with new eyes. A gift for a bride. Suddenly, the one-room building took on the aspects of a romantic haven. She could picture Aaron carrying her across the threshold to their bed. He would spend hours re-learning her body and she... had no business fantasizing about something better left in the past. She shook her head, cheeks heating. "It must have been hard back then, a young bride in the back of beyond."

He straightened, an indefinable look passing between them. "Too much for you, princess?"

She frowned. "This isn't about me, but if you must know, yes. I would find it difficult to live as they did." Her horse sidestepped, picking up on the increased tension, and Aaron ducked under his horse's neck to grasp the bridle. He probably didn't want to rescue her again. "I like my amenities."

He took his time tying the reins to the porch railing before turning to help her from the saddle. The moment his hands clasped her waist, air filled her lungs like twin balloons, not releasing until she had her feet on the ground and could take some much-needed steps away.

"Th... thank you," she stuttered, suddenly realizing just how alone they were. "Are you going to show me the inside?" She nodded toward the house, though the thought of entering the cabin and maybe seeing the bed made her stomach flutter.

Then he shook his head and she had to deal with the disappointment. "No time today—the dance, remember? Besides, it's tradition to bring Shaughnessy brides here and that's not going to be you, is it?"

The bitterness in his voice reminded her of all that had gone wrong in their relationship. A series of misunderstandings she could never rectify—didn't even know how to start. It was too late for them. All she could do was some damage control in the form of curtailing her father's activities and introducing Aaron to his daughter. The reason they were here today.

She drew her phone from her pocket and was dismayed to see only one bar. "Is there a place I can get better reception?" She glanced up in time to register the disgust on Aaron's face. "I *need* to make this call." He'd understand in a moment—if she could gain a connection.

"Yeah, sure, whatever. Try from up on the porch. Matt installed some new signal towers after he and Cassandra got stranded here, but it's still tough because of the canyon walls."

He started to walk away—to give her privacy, presumably—and she called him back. "Don't go; this concerns you as well." He hesitated, then climbed the stairs to wait near the door. Now that she was about to take this first step, her heart raced, and her palms were so clammy she could barely hang onto the phone. Aaron's presence hung over her, casting a pall on what was normally an uplifting call. Then Sarah answered on video call and she thrust him to the back of her mind, excited to see her baby.

"Hi, I thought I'd miss you today. Sorry I'm late," she said. "How is everything going?"

Sarah turned the camera to span the disaster zone that was her living room. "Good. I think we have the next generation of designers here. They've totally redecorated the house." She laughed in good humor. "And what about you? Did you mend any bridges with that cowboy of yours?"

"Shh," Trish whispered, throwing an embarrassed glance over her shoulder. Aaron cocked an eyebrow. Damn, he looked fine in jeans. She turned her back on him. "Umm, that's sort of why I'm calling. Is Madeline awake?"

The sparkle faded from Sarah's eyes. "Are you sure about this?"

Surprisingly, she was. "It's time," she said.

Sarah nodded. "For what it's worth, I think you're making the right decision. Hang on, I'll go track down your bundle of joy."

Trish swallowed over the lump in her throat and turned to Aaron. "Ready to meet your daughter?"

AARON'S THOUGHTS SCATTERED. He'd been leaning against the wall, enjoying the view of Trish's butt in a pair of skintight blue jeans, her long blond hair damn near reaching the small of her back, when she spoke the words he'd dreamed of hearing. *Meet your daughter.* For a moment he couldn't move for fear of his legs giving out, but anticipation gave him the strength to join Trish and accept the cell phone with a view of... the ceiling?

"Sarah will be right back," she said from the region of his elbow. "She just went to track the monkey down."

The love in her voice brought an ache to his chest. Did he have the right to disrupt their lives this way? Maybe it would be better if he stayed in the shadows— the father who never shows up for recitals or birthdays, but always sends a gift. Yeah, he could do that. It would break his heart, but he could do it. He would.

He tried to hand Trish the phone. "I can't," he said. "You talk to her. She'll want to see her mother."

She cocked her head and stared at him until he could practically feel her burrowing into his psyche. "What?" he snapped. "I'm not ready, okay?" He couldn't help it, his gaze kept returning to the phone as though his daughter was stretching through the air waves to reach him.

"You never asked why I had Madeline early," Trish said softly. Everything inside of him tightened at the bleak look that came into her eyes. "I was having bad headaches and abdominal pain, so I made an appointment with the prenatal doctor. After some tests they found I had developed a condition called Preeclampsia. I had to rest, drink water, see the doctor more often." Her smile was heartbreaking. "None of it helped. The placenta wasn't getting enough blood. I was basically starving our child."

Aaron couldn't bear the pain she carried like a lead weight on her shoulders. He should have been there. It stung that he hadn't, but now was not the time for recriminations. He set the phone on the railing and gathered her into his arms, ignoring how right it felt. "What happened? I mean she's here, so you obviously came through it without any ill effects, right?" *Please God, and all that is holy.*

She gazed up at him with moist eyes. "The doctor decided it would be best to induce labor. Madeline was born at thirty-six weeks. She was diagnosed with RDS—respiratory distress syndrome—and admitted into NICU for a couple of weeks. I was so scared, Aaron. I wanted to call you every day."

He stared down at the woman he'd thought he knew better than himself at one time and tried not to lose his shit. They could have died. While he'd been home licking his wounds and acting like a spoiled kid who'd had his favorite toy taken away, she'd been fighting for the life of her child. It was hard to compute. Why *hadn't* she phoned him? She must know he would have followed her to the ends of the earth, he'd been that far gone on her.

"Why didn't you call me?" he asked, his voice hoarse.

Her lashes dropped, creating an impregnable wall

between them. "I'd ended our relationship so abruptly; I didn't think you'd ever want to see me again."

He hadn't, not at first. But then the questions started; why did she leave without explanation? Was it something he'd done wrong? He'd been too angry and proud to go after her—and now he wished with all his heart he had. He tipped her chin so he could look at her precious features. "Babe, whatever else that happens between us, I will always... always be there if you or Madeline needs me. Okay?"

Her beautiful sea-green eyes opened and her lips parted on an answering *okay*, and he was lost. Swooping, his mouth closed over hers. The taste and feel made him weak and superhero strong all at the same time. He cradled her face, angling his head for a deeper connection. Hunger and need competed with longing and the urge to protect this woman from anyone who threatened her—even himself. *Mine.* He had no right to feel this way, but there it was; all the days and months without her dissolving under the tsunami of sensations she'd released in his chest. *Life-changing.* A groan escaped, maybe hers, maybe his. Her hands were everywhere, clutching his hair, clenching his shoulders, clawing his back. Claiming him even as he sought to brand her with his kisses.

He leaned back to admire her heaving breasts, the dark tumult of her eyes—emerald deep now and swimming with desire—the lush pink fullness of her lips. He'd done that. His chest swelled even as his body hardened. He ached to walk her through the door to the cabin and take her on the deep feather mattress covering the double bed his grandfather had built.

And that drew him up short.

They'd been down this road before—had a child to prove it. If there was the smallest chance of starting over with Trish, he had to do it right this time. Prove there was more to this relationship than sex, though that was off the charts good. Great even.

He grinned and Trish lost some of her glow. "What's so funny?"

"Can't a guy smile while he's holding a pretty gal?" He shouldn't tease her, but damn she was cute when she was annoyed.

"Aaron..."

Before she could tear a strip off of his hide, a faint "Hello?" turned their gazes to the cell phone resting on the aged wood of the railing. Tension raced up his spine and froze his breath as Trish reached for the device. Her eyes asked if he was going to step up to the plate or run for the hills. He replied by stepping closer and wrapping an arm around her waist, hoping he was the only one who knew how much he needed her strength for this all-important first meeting.

She gave him an encouraging smile before focusing on the caller. "Let me guess; they were playing hide and seek, right?"

Her friend Sarah, a pretty brunette, laughed. "She was hiding in the closet with Dan's shirt on her head." She lifted a chubby little bundle of arms and legs, resting

93

the little girl on her hip. "Maddie, look who's on the phone; it's Mommy."

Trish blew Madeline a kiss. "Hi, Maddie. How's Mommy's girl?"

When she heard her mother's voice, Madeline quit trying to wriggle free and turned. "Mommy?" She pulled the phone in Sarah's hand closer until the screen filled with big blue eyes. "Mommy, home," followed by a bunch of unintelligible mumbling while she ground the cell into her cheek.

Sarah managed to loosen her grip and held the instrument out so they both could see. "Like this, Maddie. There's Mommy, and...?" Her brow rose as she took in Aaron's arm holding Trish close.

Trish blushed a becoming pink but held her place, which he was immensely grateful for. Words hardly ever failed him—ask his siblings—but in this moment, when it mattered the most, he came up tongue-tied. *Lovely.*

Thankfully, Trish filled the gap. "Maddie, Mommy will be home soon. But first, I want you to meet someone." She turned the silent, judgmental eye of the camera in his direction. "This is your daddy."

Sarah sucked in an audible breath. He could relate, if only he could breathe. *Say something, idiot.* "I like hide and seek, too. Maybe we can play one day." Trish squeezed his waist, so he kept talking. "I live on a big farm. We have horses and cows and dogs and cats. Do you like kitties, Madeline?" He wanted to buy her the moon and stars but was willing to start with a house pet, if Trish would allow it.

"Kitty, kitty," his daughter chanted. "Kitty, Daddy."

Aaron's eyes filled with tears. Two little words and his heart threatened to burst. He was a father. Lord knows, the road ahead wouldn't be easy, but by damn, this little blue-eyed, blond-haired child had just shown his cynical soul that miracles can occur.

As he listened to Trish finish up the call with Sarah and reassure Maddie she wouldn't be gone much longer, he made plans. It was time to win the hearts of his girls.

15

F ive hours later, Trish arrived at the barn dance with her parents and Kyle, who seemed sober for once. They'd ridden on a hay wagon, and while she'd enjoyed the experience, her mother complained the entire trip.

"Why in the world would they expect us to dress up for this... this affair, and then make us smell like horses?"

Kyle laughed. "It's better than cow sh—"

"Kyle, please." Trish had seen a side to her fiancé this trip that she would never have accredited to the polished city businessman she'd planned to wed. Not anymore. The moment she had a chance to speak with him privately, she'd end the engagement. It would be impossible to marry him with all these feelings for Aaron raging under her skin. She didn't even know if he was willing to give her a second chance—they hadn't talked about it—but she had to try. The heart wanted what the heart wanted, and Aaron Shaughnessy was her destiny. She'd been fooling herself into believing she could move on without him all these months. It was time to fight for her man. And that began with her father.

"Daddy..."

"Not now," he said irritably. "Can't you see your mother is in distress?"

When wasn't her mother in distress? That was a better question. She accepted the hand of a waiting cowboy and used the steps he'd moved into place at the back of the wagon. After thanking him, she took in the splendor of the evening. The velvet sky made a beautiful background for the barn, dressed like a grand old dame with a multitude of lanterns and fairy lights spilling from the open doors and windows to light their way. Wide streamers hung from the rafters and guests wandered from table to table chatting while a country-western band, hired from the city, warmed up on a raised stage at the back of the hall.

So different from the sullen silence of her family.

Just for a moment, she imagined arriving at the party with the Shaughnessys and Aaron as her fiancé. She caught sight of him by the entrance greeting new arrivals and her pulse stuttered. She'd never seen him in a suit before. The charcoal gray jacket highlighted the width of his shoulders, while a crisp white shirt deepened the dark tan from hours spent in the Texas sun. A warm smile changed his face from handsome to breath-stealing. And then he noticed her standing by the wagon and it was as though everyone else faded away.

He broke from the group he'd been talking to and strode down the path, his long legs eating the distance between them. Trish met him halfway, his eyes a magnetic forcefield drawing her to his side.

"Hi," she murmured, suddenly shy.

He took her hand. "You look... beautiful."

The admiration in his expression made up for her indecision on what to wear for this all-important event. She'd only brought a few formal outfits, and none seemed to fit the occasion. She'd planned to wear a sleek black slip dress and asked Sophia for her opinion—thank goodness, because the frilly, fun concoction she'd come up with was perfect for a country farm dance.

"You don't look so bad yourself," she said. But then, Aaron was a man that women took notice of, no matter what he wore. It made her wonder if he had someone in his life now. Her stomach cramped at the thought.

"What's with the frown lines?" he asked, dropping her hand to run a gentle finger across her brow.

She closed her eyes for a moment to absorb his touch. His skin was calloused. She shivered in reaction, imagining his hands on other parts of her body.

"Chilly?" he asked, a dark smile in his voice. He knew what he did to her, damn him.

She opened her eyes and was immediately swept into the fire of his gaze. "Aaron..."

"There you are." Kyle's arm snaked around her waist,

dragging her roughly against his side. "Did you forget who you arrived with?"

He said it as a joke, but the feel of his fingers digging into her side told her he was furious. Instead of accepting the abuse, she pried herself free and took a couple of steps away from both men. "I'm well aware of my responsibilities, Kyle. If you'll excuse me, I must see to my parents." Aware she was leaving her past and present on a collision course, she fled. Not so brave after all.

AARON WATCHED as Trish hurried down the trail to where her father was helping her mom alight from the hayride. It was almost as though she was running away— from him or the idiot boyfriend?

"You need to back off," Kyle said, a smile on his face and anger brewing in his eyes.

Aaron's spine stiffened. "You don't know what you're talking about. Mind your own business."

Kyle leaned closer. "You Shaughnessys think you're so smart. Too bad this time you're doomed to fail." He shoved his hands into his pockets and whistled as he casually walked up the path and entered the barn without bothering to check on his fiancée.

What the hell was that supposed to mean? Aaron stared after the creep until he disappeared from view. What Trish saw in that guy he couldn't imagine. But then again, she'd given him a chance too, and look how that turned out.

He searched for her at the bottom of the hill. Her pretty white dress with sprigs of flowers glowed under the light of a full harvest moon. His pulse had jumped like that of a teenage kid's when she'd arrived. The dress left her shoulders bare and all he'd been able to think about was kissing her there to see if her skin was smooth as it looked. It had only been a few short days, but all the old feelings had come rushing back and he didn't know if he could box them up again—or if he even wanted to.

Trish was holding her mom's arm while her father seemed to be arguing with Rico who'd driven the wagon. Sighing, Aaron started down the hill to join them, his grandma Maddie's words ringing in his ears, *"You are a gentleman, make sure you act like one."* It would be easier if he didn't have to face the man he'd reneged on a multi-million dollar deal with, but such was life.

"Mr. and Mrs. Sylvester, Trish. Could I accompany you inside?" He held out his elbow for the elderly woman to grasp, conscious of Trish's grateful glance.

Mrs. Sylvester smiled from watery blue-green eyes like her daughter's. "Why, thank y—"

Dave Sylvester pushed between them, his discord with the farmhand forgotten. "I can handle my wife, Shaughnessy. I believe you've done enough to ruin this family, don't you?" He roughly yanked his wife forward, ignoring her pained gasp.

"Daddy," Trish beseeched, twin red flags riding her cheeks. "You promised."

"Gah," he growled and waved her off as they continued up the hill.

Aaron stared after them, shocked by the open hostility. Why had they agreed to Sophia's invitation if they hated him that much? "Your dad doesn't pull any punches, does he?"

Trish wrung her hands. "I'm sorry, Aaron. He had no right to talk to you that way."

Aaron cupped her elbows, turning her to face him. "He acted like any father should to the guy who'd made his daughter pregnant and didn't stand by her." He forced a smile. "Good thing he didn't produce a shotgun, or we might be getting hitched right now."

"I've never seen him like this. It worries me," she admitted.

Not knowing what else to say, he pulled her in for a hug but even the jasmine-fresh scent of her hair against his chin couldn't erase the ugliness of the previous moments.

16

The party was well under way by the time Trish entered the old barn with Aaron. She was angry and embarrassed on behalf of her family, so it was with some relief that she found the room packed with laughing, chattering people, her father lost in the crowd. There was an eclectic mix of styles, everything from country chic to city sleek and best of all, everyone mingled together—class and distinction had no place in this hall. The four-piece band had couples already on the dance floor. They were playing an upbeat country-western tune at the moment, unfamiliar to Trish but a hit with the crowd according to the swaying bodies.

Aaron leaned close, his breath against her cheek sending delicious shivers down her spine. "My family have a table against the far wall. Follow me."

He took her hand and led her through the throng, tipping his hat to people he knew along the way. Trish could feel the curiosity in their gazes, but for once she didn't care what people thought. The festive atmosphere was seeping into her skin, tempting her to forget—at least for tonight—her responsibilities and just have fun. She'd worry about the consequences later.

The Shaughnessy clan sat at a long wooden table with a bench along the wall and a colorful mixture of mismatched chairs marching down the other side. A red and white checkered runner ran down the center of the table decorated with pillar candles, gourds and miniature pumpkins. Snacks ranged from platters of nachos and pretzels to vegetables and dip. Everyone seemed to have either a glass of wine or bottle of beer, except Sophia, who nursed a can of iced tea.

She looked up and smiled at their approach. "I was wondering where my partners in crime were. Now, we can celebrate." She patted the bench beside her. "This place looks fabulous. I can't tell you how much it means to me. You and Aaron have managed to put Shaughnessy Guest Ranch on the map."

"Hey, sis. Take care of my date here while I go find us a drink, will you?" Aaron was gone before Trish could correct him. Her cheeks warmed even as she shook her head. "I just helped out a little, the rest is all you. The business is *going* to be a success, Sophia, mark my words."

"Date, huh?" Sophia smirked.

Aaron returned to the table and passed her a glass of wine, saving Trish from an awkward reply. "Plenty of time to talk business tomorrow, tonight's about having fun." He grinned as Matthew pulled Cassandra onto the dance floor, followed by lanky Rico and a laughing Consuela. "See?"

He stood again and held out his hand to Trish. "Dance with me?"

Helpless to say no to those mesmerizing eyes, she shrugged off Sophia and Tony's knowing smirks, and rose. Her head and her heart warred with each other; her brain thumping out a danger beat while love songs crooned in her breast. She ignored the annoying tempo and moved into Aaron's strong arms. It felt as though she'd come home.

"It's been a long time," he said, and she could see the tension in his jawline. "I'd forgotten how well we fit together."

Had he? Not her. She remembered everything about their time together. The music began—a waltz—and the other couples faded away. Trish laid her cheek against his chest, closed her eyes and let the tune sweep them into a world of their own. He'd always been a wonderful dance partner, light on his feet, responsive to the music, strong. Supportive. She'd known he would have stood with her against her father, even at the expense of his family. She couldn't allow that to happen, so she'd walked away. But it had cost her. Now, with the benefit of hindsight, she wished she'd taken a different path, made a better choice. But it wasn't too late. After the dance tonight, she planned to end her engagement and tell the truth. Her father would see it as a betrayal, she understood that.

Hopefully, with time, he would come to accept her decision. Either way, she needed to do what was best for Maddie, and—she opened her eyes and met Aaron's intent gaze—herself.

"What are you thinking about?" he asked, brushing a kiss next to her lips.

Her pulse jumped, her thoughts and his touch a combustible combination. "Us," she answered, surprising them both with her honesty. "I want us to have another chance, Aaron. I've missed you so much. Can you ever forgive me?"

His eyes flared with triumph and his hold tightened, crushing her against his ribs. "You don't know how often I've dreamed of you coming back to me." He stopped, right there in the middle of the dance floor, and clasped her face in his beloved hands. "Are you serious, baby? Be sure, because I can't go through losing you again."

Her throat squeezed shut, emotion making it hard to breathe. She'd known he'd been hurt, but to have his pain, right there in front of her, broke her heart. She'd done this to them. Not her father. Her.

Never again.

"I promise," she whispered, tears leaking from the corners of her eyes.

He leaned in and gently kissed the moisture away. "Don't cry, honey. Please, don't cry. We're going to be okay now. A family." He wrapped his arms around her, cradling her with his warmth.

A family. She was almost scared to believe it for fear

it would be swept away. She leaned back, determined to tell him everything before she made it public. "Aaron, there's something..."

"Aaron Michael Shaughnessy?" a voice boomed, the sound carrying throughout the congested room.

Aaron stiffened, his head swiveling toward the open doors. "Who wants to know?"

The crowd parted, revealing a tall, muscular man making his way toward them flanked by... Kyle, Andy, and her parents? What was going on?

Aaron took a step forward, using his body to protect hers. His brother, Rico and Tony appeared, taking up positions on either side of him. Trish's stomach lurched. Sophia grasped her arm and tugged her out of the way and she cried out, desperate to find out what was happening.

"Shush," Sophia warned. "Just listen, so we can get help, if needed."

Aware she was making sense, it nonetheless went against every instinct Trish had. She should be there, at his side. What had her father done?

"What's going on, Sheriff?" Matthew asked, his expression forbidding.

The crowd had gone silent, everyone waiting with bated breath for the sheriff's reply.

"I'm sorry to interrupt your shindig, but new evidence has come forward in the horse thief case," he said, his gaze hard as it rested on Aaron.

"Couldn't it wait?" Aaron said. "This is a special cele-
bration."

The sheriff pulled a set of handcuffs from his back
pocket. "Not this time. Aaron Shaughnessy, you are
under arrest."

17

Dumbfounded, Aaron allowed the sheriff to drag his arms behind his back—a man he'd known and considered a friend since childhood—and snap the cold silver cuffs on his wrists, pinching his skin. In his peripheral vision, he saw Matt's move to stop Stan and was thankful when Tony held him back. Bad enough one Shaughnessy was going to see the inside of a jail cell—his father would be so proud.

"What in the *hell* do you think you're doing?" Matt roared. Aaron flinched, never having heard his brother so angry.

Stan gripped his forearm to lead him through the troubled crowd. "Don't make this harder than necessary, Matthew. You can come to the station in the morning, after we get Aaron booked, and see about bail. Okay, everyone," he waved the gathering back, "give us room, please." His deputies fanned out to clear the way, leaving Aaron face-to-face with Trish's father.

The satisfied expression the man wore raised his hackles. It couldn't be coincidental the one person who wanted to see the ranch fail stood between him and freedom.

Anger surged. Aaron lunged forward, ignoring the sheriff's commands, the burning in his arms, everything in order to get into his nemesis's face. "I hope it's worth it, old man. There are some choices in life you can never take back."

After that, everything became a kaleidoscope of scenes; leaving the Harvest dance surrounded by the type of armed guards he could do without, landing hard in the rear seat of the squad car as his family and friends surged down the hill, getting read the Miranda warning with strobe lights flashing a garish red and blue against the backdrop of the old barn. But Trish's frightened face as they pulled away stayed with him the longest. He turned and watched her out the back window until they were out of sight, fiercely glad his family had surrounded her in a protective circle. He was worried sick. He knew her father had something to do with his arrest. Who would she believe?

Had he lost her love and trust forever?

He faced front and glared at the back of Stan's head through the wire cage. "You want to tell me what the hell just happened back there?"

Stan glanced over his shoulder, then focused on the

narrow country road leading away from the hacienda. "I'm not supposed to get into the details, but I'll say this; it's mighty damn convenient how a video of you *supposedly* tampering with fencing and then loading animals into a trailer fitting the description of the one we're searching for, appears just as your grand opening party for the guest house takes place. Mighty suspicious."

Pissed now, Aaron leaned forward, his arms crying at the abuse. "I'm the one who turned in the original report. Why would I do that if I was trying to rob my *own* ranch?"

"I'm not saying it makes sense, I'm just laying out the facts. It's up to the judge to determine your innocence. Now sit back and relax. Stewing won't do anyone any good."

Left with little choice, Aaron slouched in his seat and watched the fields race by in the moonlight. He'd planned on asking Trish to give him a second chance tonight. She *had* to know he was innocent, didn't she? He'd dreamed of having a family of his own with her and Madeline. He'd watched his big, somber brother mellow thanks to Cassandra and little Pippa. And now with Sophia and Tony expecting their first child, it had made him ache in unexpected ways. He'd always pictured himself as the free-flying Shaughnessy, unwilling to be tied down by ranch duties like Matthew, yet now the challenges of creating a success out of his family's legacy had become one he'd embraced without even realizing it.

Last year, when Matthew vetoed his idea for selling

his share of the property to the Sylvester Corporation in order to give the ranch a much-needed cash infusion he'd been hurt and angry. Matt bred Andalusians and Sophia was handling the books at the time—he'd felt... useless. But then he'd come up with his concept for irrigation and knew he was making a real contribution to the land and everything changed. Now this.

"Don't suppose you serve dinner in that joint, huh?" he asked. "I didn't get a chance to eat before you made your grand entrance."

Stan chuckled. "I'm sure we can rustle something up, though maybe rustle isn't the right word."

"Ha, ha, you're a riot." Aaron's smiled faded. "Thanks, man. I appreciate the heads-up on the charges. As soon as bail is posted, I'll call a buddy of mine who's a tech geek. If my lawyer can get his hands on a copy of that video, we can prove it's been rigged, and I think we both know by whom."

Stan nodded. "You've made yourself a powerful enemy, buddy. It'll be interesting to see just how far he's willing to take this thing."

Yeah, real interesting.

TRISH HUGGED herself and watched the police car drive away through teary eyes. They'd been having such a lovely day together with the ride out to his great-grandparents cabin and the dance; why did this have to happen? He was innocent, of course. This was some sort of awful mistake. Something they could laugh about later. She turned and looked for her father and found Kyle instead.

She squeezed Sophia's hand. "I'm going to fix this, I promise."

Sophia's eyes were bright with unshed tears. "He's going to *jail*, Trish. How can you fix that?"

Trish didn't know, but she was sure her father could. "I'll be right back." She slipped between Aaron's brother and Sophia's husband and made her way across the crowded lawn, aware of the knife-like gazes burrowing into her back. She couldn't blame anyone, the Shaughnessys were liked and admired—it was her family who were the outsiders.

Kyle's smirk as she approached filled her with trepidation. "The boyfriend didn't look so happy, darling," he said, making it clear he'd seen them together and didn't much care. Well, she'd known he was marrying her for her connections, not for any misplaced feelings. At least it would make ending their relationship easier.

"What did you do, Kyle?" He was almost certainly not the brains behind framing Aaron, but he might be her best bet for trapping her father in his deception. Her stomach churned at the thought of betraying her family.

He surprised her by catching her close as though greeting a lover. Strong arms made a joke of her struggles. He grazed wet lips over her cheek and whispered in her ear. "Hold still or I'll make it worse for lover-boy."

She shuddered, repulsed by his touch. What had she ever seen in him? He smelled like a brewery, his cruelty on full display. "Let me go this minute," she growled, her entire body pulsing with fury.

"Or what?" He snickered. "You'll call Daddy? I have news for you, sweetheart, he's on my side." He grasped her arm hard enough to bruise and led her into the darkness, away from the bright lights of the party and safety. When they got to the back of the barn, he dropped his hand and leaned against the wall. "You can run if you want, but I'd suggest you hear me out first."

Trish panted and rubbed the sore arm, her pulse pounding in her ears. "Touch me like that again and I'll scream the house down."

He chuckled. "Oh, I don't think you will. See, I happen to know something that could send your old man to jail for a long time. Maybe longer than he can afford—after all, he's not in the best of health, is he?"

She stared at him. "What are you talking about? My father is healthy as a... a horse." Kyle was playing with her, that had to be it. She'd know if there was more to his lies, wouldn't she? Her father seemed fine; tired, but then he'd been working on a big merger the last few months, so she'd assumed that was the reason. What if there was more to it than that? What if Kyle was telling the truth? Her stomach plummeted.

Kyle straightened and stalked toward her, a sleek jungle cat after his prey. "If you didn't spend so much time spoiling that brat, you might see what's right in front of that pretty little nose." He reached out and gave the appendage a not-so-gentle tap.

She slapped his hand away and took a step back, teetering on the edge of the slope down to the road the sheriff had taken. "What do you want, Kyle? You and I are through. I don't know why I agreed to marry you in the first place, you're a rude, obnoxious man." She was done with his games, time to find her dad.

His eyes flashed. He grabbed her arms and shook, rattling her teeth together. "You don't get to threaten me, you dumb bitch. I've worked too hard to seal this deal for dear old dad, I deserve a little compensation. Our marriage will ensure I get what's coming to me."

She froze at his words, her head reeling. It all made a sick kind of sense now. Her father's insistence on this so-called *family* adventure to the ranch, the trouble Sophia was having with advertising, the horse thieves and Aaron's subsequent framing—her father and his hunger for the Shaughnessy land was behind all of it. She could scarcely comprehend his duplicity. She needed to talk to him, get him to see reason, stop this insanity before it went any further. Apologize to Aaron and his family and beg their forgiveness. She couldn't even think about what this was going to do to her and Aaron's chances of a relationship. He'd be glad to see their backs after this.

She tried to step to the side, out of Kyle's grasp, but he wouldn't let go. "I have to find my father," she cried. Fighting to break free, she kneed him in the groin.

Swearing, he shoved her away and bent over in

agony. Trish flailed. Her heels caught in the soft ground causing her to overbalance. She fell with a sharp cry and tumbled down the hill, arms and legs bouncing over rocks and twigs. A sudden sharp pain smacked the back of her head, and everything faded to black.

18

Sophia couldn't believe what was happening. The party she and Trish had worked so hard on was a bust. All of their guests stood in little groups speculating why one of their hosts had just been driven away in the back of the sheriff's car. She wondered the same thing herself. It was ridiculous to suggest Aaron had stolen his brother's horses—this whole thing was a nightmare.

She glanced around the lawn, unwilling to make eye contact with any curious guests, but anxious as to where Trish had disappeared to after her puzzling comment. Baby Morrison picked up on her distress and rolled inside her stomach. Sophia covered the undulating wave over her skin with trembling fingers, awed by the life she carried.

"Babe, let's get you inside. Worrying won't do you

any good. Matthew will handle this." Tony wrapped an arm around her shoulders and attempted to lead her back to the barn, but she balked.

"We're fine," she said, "feel this." She guided his hand under hers just as the baby made another roll.

Tony's eyes widened and a slow smile lit his face. "Damn, that kid's going to be a football player."

Sophia laughed. "You mean she, don't you? And I rather fancy a baseball player in the family, thank you very much."

He pulled her close and kissed her with such tenderness it brought tears to her eyes. "Boy or girl, as long as you're happy, I'll be happy."

And that was one of the many reasons she adored her husband. "I love you."

He kissed her again, the gentleness tinged with passion. "Forever," he murmured, then took her hand. "Now, are you going to let me take care of my wife and child, please?"

Sophia wanted to follow him wherever he led, but Trish had her worried. "I need to check on Trish. She was acting strange—I'm concerned what she might do."

Matthew appeared at her shoulder. "Her father is behind Aaron's arrest, we all know it." His look suggested he tarred all the Sylvesters with the same brush. "I'm following Stan into the station now. He'd better have the judge on speed dial, because Aaron is *not* spending the night in some jail cell."

Pride in Matt swelled in Sophia's chest. The two brothers might argue whether the sky was blue, but when it came down to the crunch, they were there for each other. She could almost hear Grandma Maddie saying, "Nothin' thicker than blood, child. You remember that. We Shaughnessys stick together, no matter what."

"You need a hand?" Tony asked, his palm warm on the small of her back.

Matt's gaze softened on Sophia. "No. You better take your bride home. She looks tuckered."

"That's just what I was telling her." Tony grinned.

Sophia flapped her hands in mock frustration. "I'm having a baby, women do it all the time. Don't worry so much." She turned to Tony. "Go. In case he needs the voice of reason." She was well aware Matthew had a short fuse. "I'm fine. I'll find Trish and we'll make tea for when you come home." She looked at the milling party guests. "After I say goodbye to our visitors."

Tony nodded, awareness that he'd married an independent woman shining in his eyes. "Okay, but promise you'll take it easy. We can clean this mess tom..."

"Help, help. Someone help." A cry sounded from the back of the barn.

Sophia's heart jumped. She glanced from Matt to Tony, then all three, along with most of the crowd dove into the darkness in search of the injured person.

"Where are you?" Matthew shouted.

"Here, down the hill," a woman called. "Hurry, please. She's not moving."

Matt half slid, half ran down the slope, Sophia struggling to keep up. What happened? Who was hurt? But a premonition inside told her before they reached the body lying at the bottom of the embankment.

Trish.

19

Trish woke to a pounding headache. She attempted to roll over in bed and groaned, her arms and legs on fire. What the...?

"Take it easy, dear. You've had a nasty spill." Her mother placed a cool cloth on her forehead and brushed the hair away from her face. "You're lucky nothing was broken. What in the world were you doing wandering around in the dark like that? You could have been... attacked, or something."

Trish would have smiled, but her head hurt too much. Mother always believed the worst of every situation. If one thought about it, maybe she was wise to take that strategy—at least she'd never be disappointed. "I'm sorry, Mom. I didn't mean to worry you. How long have I been... sleeping?" She hesitated to say unconscious, not wanting to upset her mother any more than she was.

"Not long. The Shaughnessy kids found you and

brought you to the hacienda. I don't know what I would have done without Consuela. She looked you over and assured your father and me you would be fine after a rest." She patted her chest, looking as pale as Trish felt. "You gave me such a fright."

Her father. It came back to her in a rush. Confronting Kyle. His ultimatum. The shove. Because that's what it had been. He'd deliberately pushed her down that hill. What kind of man did that? A psychopath, that's who.

She tried to sit up, but her head exploded in agony and she collapsed. A careful examination of the left side of her head with her fingers told her the reason; a tender area about the size of her fist, painful to the touch.

She winced and her mother tut-tutted, pulling her hand away from the injury. "Don't touch it now, you'll only make it worse," she admonished handing over a couple of pills and a glass of water. "Take these, they'll help."

Trish wanted to say no—she'd never been a fan of self-medicating—but it hurt too much to argue. She accepted the pills and swallowed them dry, not up to lifting her head again. "Thanks, Mom," she whispered. Vulnerability tightened her throat. "Where's Father?" She wiped the tears from the corners of her eyes. "I need to talk to him."

Her mother sat back, cupping the glass in her hand. "He went to our room to pack. He said now that you are injured it's time to go home. As though we should have been here in the first place," she added under her breath.

Trish stared at her. "What is that supposed to mean, Mom? The Shaughnessys have gone out of their way to make us feel welcome." *And look at how we paid them back.*

"Well, Trish, I mean really, do I look like the cowboy type to you?"

No. There were many labels she could apply to her mother; vain, pompous, snobbish, but never kind or friendly, as Trish had found country folk to be. Of the two, she knew which she preferred.

"I really need to see Father. Could you please ask him to come to my room?"

She must have looked pathetic enough, her mom rose with only minor grumbling and glided to the door. She glanced over her shoulder, a hand on the doorknob. "I hope you've come to your senses after this unfortunate incident. This is no place to raise a child." With that, she slipped out and gently closed the door.

So, she knew. Not surprising really. It was only a matter of months after her affair with Aaron that she'd admitted to her pregnancy. Tired and depressed, she hadn't raised a fuss when her father insisted on the merger with Kyle. She wished she had now. And why him? He wasn't like her dad's normal business partners, rough around the edges, arrogant. Since having Madeline, she'd come out of her funk and realized there was no way Kyle was going to have a part in her daughter's upbringing, but she hadn't had the courage to break it off —until now.

A sharp knock later, her father strode into the room. At least he had the grace to look uncomfortable with her injury.

"Father. Thanks for taking the time to see me."

"No need for sarcasm, young lady. I told your mother to stay with you until we leave." He edged closer to the bed. "How do you feel?"

She smiled wryly. "Like I rolled down a hill. Why are you leaving?"

He sat in her mother's chair and patted her hand. "Not me, all of us. How can I take care of my family among these... these criminals? Let's get you home to Madeline and let justice run its course."

Appalled, she stared at him like he'd suddenly sprouted two heads. How could he even consider leaving Aaron in jail? The father she'd liked and admired as an innocent child was nowhere to be found in the shrewd gaze of the man holding her hand.

Disgusted, she jerked free. "You're behind this, aren't you? I'm not leaving, Dad. Aaron is Maddie's father; he deserves my loyalty. I'm not exactly sure what you're up to, but if it has something to do with Shaughnessy land, forget it. Any major decisions are put to a vote at the stockholder's meeting, and since I hold a number of shares as well as the confidence of many of the members, you'd stand a good chance of being overruled. You don't want that, do you?"

Trish hated to play hardball with her own parent, but he'd left her without a choice. She had no proof that he'd staged Aaron's arrest, but something told her she was on the right track. He'd lost a lot of money when the land deal fell through last year—enough that he had to sell some of his shares in the company. Shares she and her brother had quietly bought up to keep the majority in their family. But she wasn't above using them to stop this nonsense before it went any further.

Her father's genial expression faded to irritation. He rose and paced the room, lifting a vase here and a book there. Finally, he turned and held out his hands. "What do you want from me, daughter? I need this deal. There are people who... could make life difficult if I fail."

This is what she'd been afraid of; he'd tangled with the wrong investors. "Dad, Kyle pushed me down that hill. Is he part of whatever is going on?"

He stared at her, horrified. "I... I would never condone this. You must believe me." He dropped his head into his hands.

Empathy rose, choking out the anger. He'd always run his company with firm, capable hands. The downturn in the market, some bad investments and his age had all played a part in his downfall. There had to be a way he could save face and still help Aaron.

"We'll figure it out, Dad. We're family."

aron rubbed his red wrists and glanced sideways at Matthew as he climbed behind the wheel of the ranch pickup. "Thanks for bailing me out." Something he hoped never to have to say again.

Matt eyed his hands before flicking up to his face. "I think that's a Shaughnessy first; arrested as a horse thief." He shook his head and turned the key, waiting until the truck started with a low grumble before shifting into reverse. "Want a coffee for the road?"

Aaron grimaced at the pointed barb, then nodded. "Sure, thanks. Jailhouse coffee is about as good as it sounds." Thank goodness, the county judge was an old family friend. He'd climbed out of bed long enough to sign the bail bond with a stern warning to stay in the area until the trial. No problem there, Aaron wasn't going anywhere but home.

He cleared his throat. "I know what you're thinking—"

"That the sheriff is a prick for arresting you? Yeah, he and I had words about that."

Aaron stared at him, shocked. "So you believe me?"

Matt signaled into the drive-thru of a popular coffee shop. "Trust me, bro, if I caught you stealing anything, much less ranch stock, the sheriff would be the least of your problems."

Was that a yes, then? He'd spent so many years trying to live up to his big brother's image that he'd lost his way for a while. It took losing out on the land deal, which he was grateful for now, and Trish to make him realize he wasn't Matthew. He didn't have to be perfect all the time; he just had to be himself.

He waited until Matt placed their order through the intercom before trying again. "You didn't really answer the question; do you think I took your damn horses or not?"

Matt slowly rolled the truck forward in the surprisingly long lineup for that time of night. "If you have to ask, you're dumber than I thought." He grumbled something that sounded suspiciously like, "*idiot,*" before rolling down his window to accept the drinks and a box filled with fresh-baked donuts. "Here," he said, handing the lot over to Aaron so he could get back on the road for home.

Country music played quietly as they devoured the sugary treats, then Matt sighed. "I needed that, bet you did too. Prison food as good as they say it is?" His grin held more than a touch of mockery.

"Ha, ha. You're a real riot." Aaron's shoulders eased. "So, what's next?"

Matt held up his cup. "You mean other than my coffee?" He took a satisfying slurp, returned it to the cupholder, and turned down the radio. "We're going to find out who set you up and make them sorry they tangled with a Shaughnessy, that's what."

Aaron's throat tightened. For so long he'd tried to compete for attention as the middle child in a family of overachievers, always the odd man out. Now, with a few simple words, Matt assuaged years of balled up loneliness and isolation in his gut. The resentment he'd carried like a lead weight dispersed, leaving him lighter... happier. If that's what getting arrested produced, he wished he'd done it years ago. "Thanks, man," he said around the thick ball of emotion choking him. He cleared his throat. "There's something I need to tell you." He took a drink of his coffee, trying to get his thoughts in order. "I found out the other night I'm a father—a baby girl." Saying it out loud made it seem more real somehow. He grinned at the shock on Matt's face. "I caught you off-guard. First time that's happened."

"Huh?" Matt almost missed the turn for the ranch. He cranked the wheel hard and the truck swayed alarmingly, the rear-end skidding sideways on the gravel road.

Aaron swore and grabbed the dash, his foot punching the floor in a search for the phantom brake on his side of the vehicle. "Holy shit, you trying to kill us, bro?" Once he got his heart out of his mouth and released his death-grip, he leaned back and laughed. "Whew, that got the old adrenaline pumping. I take it you're surprised."

Matthew pulled over and stopped, throwing the gearshift into park. "Are you sure? Maybe it's some woman's way of taking you for a few bucks. What does she want?"

Aaron wasn't sure if he should be insulted his brother thought so little of his choice of women friends, or amused. "Wow. So, you think the only type of woman that would go out with me is after our nebulous wealth? That hurts, man. Truly hurts."

"Always the funny guy," Matt muttered. "Seriously, there are tests out there to verify paternity. We'll book an appointment and have your... friend take the child in to authenticate her claim. If it's true, we'll figure out what to do from there."

Aaron's ire rose and fell like a deflated balloon. It was Matthew's nature to take charge, he never even considered anyone might have a different opinion—poor Pippa, she was in for a hard time growing up with him for a father.

He handed Matt his coffee and took a reviving sip of his. "It's been a long day, I guess we're both on edge." He turned to meet his brother's gaze. "The mother of my child is Trish, she told me the other night, at dinner. At first, I couldn't believe it either, but she wouldn't lie to me, Matt. The baby *is* mine."

"Well," Matt said, holding out his hand. "I guess congratulations are in order then."

Aaron grasped the hand and reeled his brother in for a heartfelt hug. "Thanks, man. I plan on asking Trish for a second chance—she's the one, you know?"

Matt leaned back, stared him in the eye, and slowly nodded. "Don't let anyone stand in your way then, buddy. The love of your life won't wait forever."

Yeah, that's what worried Aaron. They still had to get past her father and the douchebag she called a fiancé.

By the time they arrived home it was nearing midnight and the only light came from the kitchen. Aaron was tempted to sneak in through the front door and avoid his family until morning, but knew they'd be worrying about him. Besides, maybe Trish was there. He should have saved her a donut. His heart kicked up a notch and he grinned. He was acting like a lovesick fool and it felt great. This time, he was going to make sure she didn't get away. He planned to ask her to marry him. Just thinking it made his palms sweat—he had it bad.

"Looks like you have a welcoming committee," Matthew said, swinging to a stop in the courtyard.

"I noticed," Aaron admitted. "What should I say?" he asked, suddenly hit by nerves. He stared out of the windshield at the flickering lights behind the kitchen curtain. "I don't want to be a disappointment."

"Aaron." Matt waited until he had his attention. "You may be my brother, but you're an idiot. Those people in there adore the ground you walk on. There's nothing you could ever say or do to change that. Now, come on. I'm ready to tuck my wife into bed."

The kitchen was filled with the mouthwatering aroma of warm apple pie. Sophia and Consuela leaned against one side of the island and looked up, their faces bursting with joy.

"*Bueno*, you're home," Consuela cried, clapping her hands.

Tony and Cassandra turned on their bar stools, Tony holding a forkful of pie to his mouth.

Cass slid off the stool and hurried over. She hugged Aaron, then slipped under Matt's welcoming arms and gave him a lingering kiss. "I see you worked your magic."

Matt's gaze flicked to Aaron before returning to his beautiful wife. "We cast a spell over the judge, that's for sure. Got any of that pie left? Rescuing pains-in-the-you-know-where takes a lot of energy."

Cass laughed. "I think we saved a piece or two." She tightened her hold on Matt before letting go. "Come on before your sister beats you to them."

Aaron followed the lovebirds and tried to rein in his disappointment that Trish wasn't with his family. He'd hoped she would be at least somewhat worried about him sitting in a prison cell. Slight exaggeration since Stan had placed him in an interrogation room with access to a real bathroom, but still...

He suffered through Sophia's jokes and lapped up Consuela's love shown with a plate-sized slice of pie and a huge scoop of vanilla ice cream. "This *almost* makes up for tonight's horror show." He took a big bite and let the flavors explode in his mouth before winking at Consuela. "I knew I was your favorite."

As expected, his family erupted in a cacophony of protests, allowing him to eat his pie in peace. When he was done, he straightened and rubbed his full belly. "Dang, that was good. I didn't get time to eat at the dance, so this hit the spot." He looked at the suddenly serious faces. "None of that. It's over for now anyway. I was having a good time with Trish until... what?" he asked, picking up on a weird vibe in the room. He frowned at Sophia. Something was wrong. "Where's Trish?"

It was Matt who answered. "Don't freak out."

So, of course he freaked out. "What the hell is going on?" He glared at his brother. "Did you scare her away the moment my back was turned?" Inside, he knew better, but fear made him an insolent jerk.

Consuela tsked. "Did your momma and papa teach you to talk that way?" She rounded the counter and stood head to chest with Aaron. "You listen to me now. Your brother was worried sick about you, the moment he knew Miss Trish was going to be okay he jumped on the phone, called in some favors and got you out of jail. You should be thanking him, not acting like a spoiled child. You are better than this." She patted his arm and moved aside to gather the dishes.

Properly chastised, Aaron opened his mouth to apologize when the rest of what she'd said struck home. "Trish is hurt?" He headed for the hall, determined to see her, even if it was after midnight.

"Aaron, wait. There's more," Sophia called.

Impatient, he turned. "Can't it wait? I want to make sure she's all right."

"Doc stopped by to check her out. She has scrapes and bruises on her arms and legs, but he was mostly concerned with the head injury. He suggested we wake her every couple of hours throughout the night just to be safe."

Bruises? Head injury? What the hell happened after he was gone? When the sheriff arrived, they'd been in each other's arms and he'd been fantasizing of a future, complete with a white picket fence, two or three kids and Trish. Now, it seemed like a dream.

"It was that no-good fiancé of Miss Trish's," Consuela said, her hands clenched together. "He pushed her down the hill behind the big barn."

Aaron's heart stopped and then jumped madly in his chest. There were boulders lining the road at the bottom of that hill. She could have smashed her head wide open. He could have lost her forever.

He lunged for the hallway, ignoring Sophia's cry to wait. He couldn't, he had to see her with his own eyes. He'd deal with Sylvester later.

The door was ajar and a murmur of voices, one deep, one feminine, greeted him as he reached for the knob. He was about to push the door in and announce his presence when he overheard a conversation that turned his blood to ice.

"... take care of my family among these... these criminals?" Trish's father.

Words he couldn't make out, and then...

"I need this deal. There are people who... could make life difficult if I fail." Trish's father said.

Aaron strained to catch Trish's response.

"We'll figure it out, Dad. We're family."

Heart shattering into what felt like a million pieces, he turned and walked away.

21

Aaron shivered and tugged the collar of his sheepskin jacket closer around his neck. If this weather continued, they'd see a white Christmas this year—little Pippa would love that. As he turned Dickens to do one more sweep of the low-lying hills in search of newborn calves, his thoughts went to Madeline. She'd be a year old now, and no doubt driving her mother crazy trying to keep up. He'd already sent a passel of gifts and wanted to send more, but with only a week left until the holiday, he didn't hold out much hope they'd arrive on time. Sophia hounded him nonstop to deliver them in person, and Lord knows he wanted to, but Trish would probably slam the door in his face—not that he could blame her. Once again, he'd led with his heart instead of his head.

Blowing out a gusty sigh that sent an icy cloud in front of his face, he leaned over to give Dickens a pat.

"What do you say, buddy, time for a warm barn and a belly full of hay?" The horse's ears flickered, and he jangled the reins. "You drive a hard bargain, one pail of oats, but no more." Aaron grinned and swung for home.

They'd traversed half of the valley when a low cry reached them from a stand of frost-tipped mesquite. Aaron took Dickens as close as he dared, then dismounted and ground-tied the horse. "Wait here. Let's see what we've got, hmm?" He grabbed a length of rope and inched his way through the thorny growth until he found the calf caught in a hollow under a fallen log. "Now, how did you manage that? Huh, little guy?" The animal looked at him with big brown eyes and ridiculously long eyelashes and Aaron's heart melted. "Hang on, fella, we'll get you out of there. Just don't keep struggling, you'll make it worse." He kept a low, one-sided conversation going while he fashioned a slip knot into a loose loop and lowered it over the calf's neck, then tightened the knot. The poor thing was weak and shivering, no doubt dehydrated. Hard to say how long he'd been stuck. He needed care soon or they could lose him.

"Okay, you're not going to like this very much. Just hang tight and you'll be out before you know it." Aaron did what he could to deepen the trench the calf would have to follow to get free, then backed out of the bushes, catching his hair and coat on the thorns. Cows often found the most difficult areas to give birth, in the hope their babies would be protected from predators. Instead, many of them died from exposure or lack of nutrition—it was a tough situation. Which is why he'd been out here freezing his butt off for the last month; it had nothing to do with the emptiness he carried like an aching hole in his gut since Trish went back to Austin.

He tied the end of the rope to the pommel and frowned at the heavy dark clouds on the horizon. Damn if that didn't look like snow. Just what he didn't need right now. "Okay, Dickens, we're going to back up nice and easy. Give that little fella time to find his feet." He stood near his horse's head and grasped the bridle. "Let's go." Dickens put his weight on his haunches and side-stepped backward, drawing the rope taut.

"That's it, just a little farther." Suddenly, the rope went slack, indicating the calf had lunged out of the hole. "Whoa, good job, boy."

Aaron jogged to the mesquite and gently tugged the rope until the calf popped into view, scared and shaking, but free. He scooped him up and returned to Dickens' side. "Now for the fun stuff. I'm going to lay you across the saddle and you're going to stay there until I can climb up and hold you on my lap—got that?" The calf answered with a half-hearted bleat and Dickens snorted. Aaron grinned. "Good, that's settled, then."

He lifted the animal into the saddle with a grunt and kept a firm hand on his back while reaching for a stirrup so he could swing onboard himself. Once they were situated, he took the rope from around the calf's neck and made quick work of coiling it. Just as he turned to place the roll into his saddlebag a dark shape broke away from the gathering shadows. Aaron's heart jumped into his throat. He froze. A weak calf was fair game for the big cats that roamed the area, not to mention wolves. His rifle was tied behind his saddle and he contemplated his chances before they were attacked. Trish's beautiful smile flashed behind his eyes. All the things he wished he'd said and now might never have the opportunity to say. The daughter he'd never met. If only he could have a second chance.

The calf lifted its head weakly and bleated again. Aaron cursed and pressed his knees into Dickens' side, urging the horse into motion. Just as the animal's muscles bunched, a low bellow echoed across the distance. Aaron pulled up on the reins, causing Dickens to rear slightly before sliding to a quivering stop. The threat he'd been envisioning trotted into sight—the calf's mother, by the look of her.

"Whew. You just took ten years off my life, right there." He wiped his sweaty brow with a shaky hand. "Waiting on your baby here, were you? Okay then, follow us back to the ranch and we'll get both of you taken care of in the barn. Sound good?"

Once again, he squeezed Dickens' sides and kept an eye on the cow as they started off for home. Now that his mother was nearby, the calf grew restless, anxious to eat and gain back some of those lost pounds. "Soon enough, little guy. At least your story's going to have a happy ending."

Aaron wondered if his would.

MATT WAS WORKING the long rope with one of his two-year-old Andalusians when Aaron rode into the yard. A couple of hands sat on the fenced enclosure watching the exhibition but jumped down when the Charolais trotted into view. Aaron waved them away from the skittish animal. It was a bad idea to get between two thousand pounds of protective momma cow and her baby. He figured the only reason she hadn't attacked him was because she'd sensed he wanted to help.

"I got it," he called, lifting a gloved hand to his brother. "See you inside?"

Matt nodded and began to gather rope as Aaron continued through the wide-open doors of the calving barn. The season had just begun, so only a couple of the stalls were occupied. He chose one near the back, hoping it would be a quiet haven for the stressed animals.

Dickens, trained to be calm around the massive Charolais, stood still while Aaron dismounted and carried his precious burden into the clean stall. He laid the calf in a bed of straw and moved back, giving Mom plenty of space to check on her infant. It didn't take long for the calf to clamber to its feet and search out Momma's teat.

Aaron watched to make sure the cow would accept her baby, then edged his way out and closed the stall door. "Well, we did it, buddy. Feels kind of good, don't it?" He rubbed Dickens' forehead and straightened his long black bangs. "Give me a minute to get these two sorted and then it's your turn, I promise."

"I'll take your horse over and get started while you finish here. Another stray?" Matthew strode down the aisle, his burnished blond hair glinting under the bare light bulbs high over their heads.

Aaron waited for him to draw closer before handing over his reins. "Yeah. Found him in a hollow east of Hidden Valley. Momma there scared the living hell out of me—thought she was a cougar, at first."

Matt raised his brow and chuckled. "If we had cougars that size, I'd be scared too."

Aaron's ears heated. "Ha, ha. What happened to your hat, horse throw you?" If there was one thing Matt prided himself on—other than gambling—it was his prowess with horses. He was a born equestrian; it was no wonder he'd turned to it as a career.

"Pippa borrowed it to play cowboy and fell on it, with a glass of juice," he admitted. "Cass washed it—" they both grimaced, "and has it on a slow air dry now."

That was the end of the hat, in other words. "Your daughter is a sweetheart," Aaron said, and meant it. She was cute as a button and smart, too. Made him wonder...

"Yeah, she is, and she deserves cousins to play with. How long you going to continue moping before you fix what you broke?"

The words hit him like arrows to the heart. He glared at Matthew. "It's none of your damn business." He turned to stomp toward the bales of hay stacked in the feed room, but Matt swung him around by the arm.

"Stop right there. I've got something to say, and you're going to listen whether you want to or not." Matt's eyes pinned him in place. "What I did last year was wrong, okay? You have every right to do whatever you want with the land that was deeded to you. I stood in the way of your success and for that, I am truly sorry. It cost you your woman and your happiness." He ran a hand through his hair before meeting Aaron's narrowed gaze. "Look, I can't do anything about the past, but I'm sure as hell not going to stand by while you screw up your future.

"Trish called me last week. She knows you were there, in the hall, that night. She tried to find you the next day, but you were long gone. I know you're hurt, but so is she, bro. You need to give her a chance to explain. Do you really want to live with yourself if you don't?"

Aaron blinked the moisture from his eyes. Sometime on the ride home with that stubborn cow and her calf, he'd already decided he was going to Austin to find his girl. What got to him now was Matthew. His brother truly cared about his happiness. The feeling was indescribable. Love filled his chest to overflowing. Brotherly love.

He surprised Matt with a bear of a hug and a rough pat on the back. "Thanks, man. Appreciate the advice, even though I'd figured it out already. I'd planned to leave for the city in the morning—if you can spare me?"

Matt's face split into a wide, white smile. "About

damn time," he said. "Oh, and by the way, we have a big-time investor for the ranch—a silent partner. You might want to thank your girlfriend for that, too."

Nervous anticipation tightened Aaron's gut. This would be the biggest gamble of his life. Matthew seemed to think he'd be welcomed in Trish's home. He prayed his brother wasn't wrong.

22

Trish tucked the fuzzy princess blanket around her daughter's waist, kissed her rosy cheek, and gave the swing another push, smiling at the resultant giggles. Rosewood Park was quiet today, maybe because it was so close to Christmas. The eastern suburb on the outskirts of Austin was a hub for young families who had opened their arms to her and Madeline after they'd moved out of her parents' home on their return from the ranch. It terrified her to have sole responsibility for her daughter's health and wellbeing, but she hadn't felt like she had a choice.

At least the three-bedroom split-level she'd found on a quiet residential street was comfortable and had a fenced backyard. So far, she'd worked from home, but that was temporary. Sooner or later, she was going to have to interview candidates for daycare—something she wasn't looking forward to.

"Momma, Momma," Maddie chanted, clapping her hands in glee.

"Okay, pumpkin. Once more and then it's time to go home and plug in our Christmas tree. We need to let Santa know where you are, because someone was a good girl this year."

"Goo' girl, goo' girl." Maddie swayed in the child swing. "Go, Momma, go." She'd discovered her voice in the last couple of months and liked to parrot everything she heard, sometimes to her mother's embarrassment.

Trish waved to a young couple with a stroller that she'd met in the park a few times walking along the pathways. They lifted their hands in return and continued on their way arm-in-arm. Melancholy threatened and she forced it back down. Sometimes, life didn't turn out the way one hoped. All you could do is roll with the punches and keep on dreaming. Good advice; the trick was following it.

"Time to go, Maddie-boo." She stopped the slowing swing and unfastened the safety strap before lifting the wriggly-worm out of her seat. "Quit, or I'm going to drop you," she warned. If only they could bottle that energy.

"Need a hand?" A familiar voice asked.

Trish froze in the act of placing her baby in the stroller. *Aaron.* Aaron was here. Her pulse fluttered wildly as she slowly straightened and turned, Maddie a safety net in her arms. He stood near the kids climbing wall, tall and lean and so handsome he took her breath away.

"I didn't scare you, did I?" he asked, removing his cowboy hat a touch nervously as he closed the distance between them. "You're looking good, Trish. Real good."

Caught off balance, she reacted with anger. "Why are you here, Aaron. We have nothing to say."

He flinched slightly before nodding toward Madeline, his expression miserable. "Did you get the gifts I sent?"

She felt the tiniest crack in her armor and fought to shore it up. "You can't buy her love, you know." Her arms tightened around her daughter until Maddie squirmed.

Aaron's lips quirked, his eyes dark with pain. "You're not going to make it easy for me, are you?" His gaze was drawn to Maddie again. "Can I hold her?"

Trish instinctively turned aside, then grudgingly nodded. "She doesn't do well with strangers," she warned, then wished she hadn't when Aaron recoiled. When did she become such a bitch?

In an effort to make the transition easier for her daughter—the only one who mattered, she lied to herself —she forced a smile. "Maddie, want to meet Daddy?"

Madeline stared at the man with eyes so like her own. Whatever she saw must have reassured her because she reached out with both hands, her body leaning toward him with all her might. "Daddy, Daddy."

Aaron's mouth dropped in wonder as he accepted the precious burden. "Well hello, Maddie-girl. Aren't you just the prettiest filly in all of Texas?" Matching dimples appeared, father and daughter, as they grinned at each other.

Trish's eyes filled with tears—so much time wasted. She should never have kept her pregnancy a secret. Madeline had a right to have the love of both parents.

Aaron noticed her tears and misinterpreted them. He tried to hand Maddie back, but she wasn't having any of it.

She wrapped her arms around his neck and held on like a little monkey. "Stay, Daddy. Stay."

Helpless, he took Trish's hand. "Don't cry, baby. It'll be all right. I only came to see if we could have another chance, but if it's going to hurt you like this, I'll leave."

Another chance? Even after everything they'd been through, he was willing to work things out? Her heart began to soar, but before she could accept what he was saying she had to tell him the truth.

She cupped their clasped hands together and squeezed. "I don't want you to leave. Maddie needs her father and I... I love you, Aaron Shaughnessy, but I need to explain about my dad—"

He tugged until she fell against his side. He wrapped his arm around her waist, snuggling her into a loving family circle. "It doesn't matter. Matthew told me about the investor. I don't know how to thank you for rescuing not just me, but our family business, as well." He touched her lips in a kiss she felt to the bottom of her toes. "I love you, Trish Sylvester. I always have. Thank God, you came into my life."

Jealous, Maddie placed pudgy fingers on her father's cheeks and turned his face to hers. "Kiss, kiss," she demanded.

Trish and Aaron burst into laughter as he complied. It was going to be a wonderful Christmas, after all.

*C*hristmas Morning

The Shaughnessy household at Christmas was unlike any Trish had attended. Every nook and cranny of the hacienda radiated happiness and cheer. Garlands hung from mantles and doorframes, colorful cloths decorated tables and furniture, and a truly lovely Leyland Cyprus filled a corner of the den with a multitude of twinkling lights and satin-colored balls on what seemed like every branch.

The hardwood floor under the tree had disappeared, taken over by parcels in every shape and size. They toppled one over the other like a giant's building blocks. Holiday music played from speakers built into the ceiling, and the mouth-watering aromas of bacon and sausage competed with real maple syrup and apple cider left over from their recent breakfast.

Matthew, as the eldest, sat on the floor handing out

presents, the kids at his knee, their eyes bright with excitement. It was so much more than Trish had expected that it brought tears to her eyes. Maddie accepted her new family with hardly a quibble and already followed Pippa wherever she went. Matthew, Cassandra, Sophia, Tony, and even Consuela had opened their arms and never made any mention of the sabotage committed by her family. After Kyle admitted to stealing the horses and rolled over on her father and Andy's plan to ruin the Shaughnessy name so they would be forced to sell their land, Aaron was acquitted. She'd expected him to press charges, but they'd taken the high road instead and accepted the offer her father had been encouraged to make—silent ranch investor.

And Aaron—he'd embraced fatherhood better than she'd dreamed, the connection between him and Madeline a joy to behold. She would have loved him anyway, but the fact he'd come after her even though he hadn't known about the deal she'd made with her dad? She adored him for that.

"Where's Aaron?" Sophia asked. At six months' pregnant, she looked beautiful in her red velvet jumper covered in dancing candy canes. She plopped a bright pink bow on Pippa's curly head before sinking onto the sofa next to Trish.

Trish lifted her phone and snapped a picture. "He said something about more gifts, crazy man. He should be back soon."

Sophia laughed. "He's having fun this year, it's good to see. You're a good influence."

Trish flushed. "I think it's all Madeline."

Hearing her name, Maddie glanced guiltily at her mom as she reached for Pippa's bow. Matt solved the impending argument by plucking a neon green corkscrew ribbon from another parcel and handing it to the baby. Satisfied, she dropped to the floor and worked at hooking it into her hair like her cousin's.

Sophia clasped Trish's hand. "Give yourself some credit. He's a different guy around you. Happier."

Trish's throat tightened. She hugged her friend. "When I think of what my dad planned—"

Sophia vigorously shook her head. "None of that," she admonished. "If not for you and your father we might have lost the ranch. What did Aaron say when you told him?"

"He took it better than expected. I think he was just relieved the pressure you were under is gone. He even called my father to thank him." His forgiveness meant more than she could say. It had taken a united front to hold back the shareholders and get them to agree to take a chance on Balmoral, but already they were seeing a return on their investment. The guest ranch was fully booked for the first quarter, Matt had sold two of his mares at a profit with calls coming in for more, and Aaron had received funding to further research his irrigation ideas. The tides were changing, and Trish was grateful to have helped in some small measure.

"Daddy, daddy."

Maddie's delighted squeal alerted her to Aaron's return. He'd entered without anyone noticing and stood near the door, staring at her with a diffident expression. Trish rose, her pulse going haywire.

Aaron crossed the room to stand in front of her, his eyes suspiciously bright.

Now she really was worried. "What's wrong? You're scaring me." Was it her mom? Her father?

Taking her hands in his trembling ones, Aaron dropped to one knee. Sophia gasped while Trish burst into tears. "I know we've had our share of ups and downs," he began, and everyone laughed, "but, through it all my love for you remained constant. And then you gave me the precious gift of our daughter and I realized how empty my world would be without you."

He tugged a blue velvet box from his pocket and lifted the lid to reveal a stunning solitaire diamond ring. "Trish Sylvester, I promise to love and cherish you all the days of our lives. Will you marry me?"

Maddie, tired of being ignored, flung herself into her father's arms, upsetting his grip on the box. It landed in the pile of discarded gift wrap and disappeared.

Aaron stared at her, stunned, then broke out laughing. "So much for romantic gestures."

"No one move," Consuela called, already beginning the search. Matt and Cassandra joined in while Tony leaned over to relieve Aaron of his girl.

"Come with Uncle Tony. I know where the candy is hidden."

Aaron kept his gaze on Trish. "You're making me sweat, here. Are you going to give me an answer? I need you, Trish."

She sank to the floor and wrapped her arms around his neck. "I love you with my heart and soul," she whispered. "You're the best thing that ever happened to me. I'd be honored to become your wife." Their lips met in a kiss filled with passion, promise and wonder. Trish melted in the heated blue fire of his eyes.

"So, is that a yes?" he murmured against her mouth.

She smiled, her world suddenly a much brighter place. "That's a *hell* yes."

AFTERWORD

These days, the ranching industry is finding it tougher and tougher to stay alive in a challenging climate.

Being an independent rancher is simply not financially attractive, and by 2012 there were 20,000 more Texas farmers age 70 or older than there were Texas farmers between the ages of 25 and 34. Aging ranchers are left with little control over what will happen to their land when they're gone, since their sons or daughters are often uninterested in continuing the ranching tradition they've inherited.

I wrote this series partially because of a love of horses,

but mainly to bring an awareness to the uncertain fate of farmers. We need this industry to survive and should be doing whatever we can to protect our pioneers and secure the land for future generations to come.

ACKNOWLEDGMENTS

I hope you enjoyed My Girl, Book 3 in the Gambling Hearts series. I've also included a small excerpt from Skating on Thin Ice- Book 1 in the Men of WarHawks series to share the beginning of Sam and Mac's story.

Reviews are the lifeblood of any successful author. Without you, we can't be heard.

If you enjoy the story, please consider sharing on your favorite social media sites, as well as GoodReads and from wherever you've bought the book.

Thank you,

Jacquie Biggar

Jacqbiggar.com

FREE DOWNLOAD!

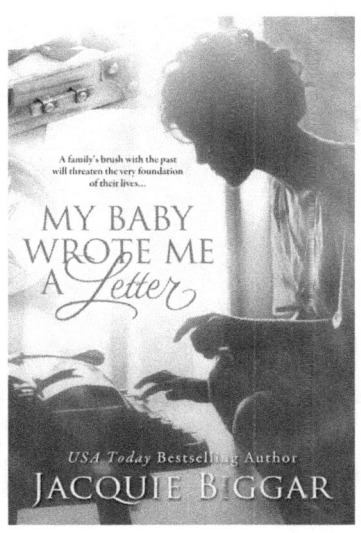

My Baby Wrote Me A Letter

A family's brush with the past will threaten the fabric of their lives.

Eight months pregnant and her Navy husband away on a mission, Grace Freeman craves the security of her childhood home in Canada.

When a letter written by her long-lost mother is found in an old writing desk it creates a tear in the fabric of her family.

Can Grace find a way to bring peace to those she loves, or will a message from the past destroy their future?

Newsletter subscribers also get bonus content and insider information every month. I love giveaways and there is lots of interesting stuff for me to share with you!

Newsletter- Sign up Now!

Mac Wanowski was having the best night of his hockey career. Two goals and three assists with a period and a half to go. Everything was going their way. He should be a shoo-in for MVP. The Victoria WarHawks were playing on home turf to a full stadium of rowdy fans with fast ice—nothing could stop him now.

The blow came out of nowhere.

One minute he was flying down the ice with the puck held in the sweet spot of his stick, the crowd roaring his name, the net in sight, in the next instant Mac was shoved from behind and smacked into the boards. He bounced and went down hard on his right knee. The pain was immediate and intense. It sucked the breath from his lungs and left him seeing stars. He dropped his head between his arms and tried to remain conscious until the medics arrived. It was small consolation the refs caught the illegal move and rang the penalty buzzer.

Fricking Murtagh.

The other team's enforcer liked to pull sneak attacks. He'd done it before. Mac rolled onto his back and blinked as the auditorium swam before his eyes.

"Wow, man, that had to hurt." Samson chortled, skidding to a stop against the boards. The plexi-glass shook with the collision.

Edwards, the team's doctor skated across the ice in his dress shoes and dropped to his side. "Hey, Hammer, nice hit. How you doing?"

"Been better," Mac grumbled. He squinted through the face-shield and yanked off his gloves. "It's the knee, Doc. Screwed it good this time." The helmet came next, clattering onto the ice along with his dreams.

"Don't worry. He will pay." Lazlo, the grinder,

towered over Mac glaring at the other team as though daring them to come near.

"Keep it clean, boys," the ref said, gliding up to pat the Croatian's arm. "I don't wanna send you to the bench, but I will." He exchanged a look with the doc, then blew his whistle and waved an arm over his head. "Gurney's on the way."

Mac growled and tried to sit up, but Edwards forced him down. The guy might be old but working around a bunch of hockey players kept him in shape. "Take it easy, Mac. It's just a precaution. You don't want to aggravate that tendon any more than you need to."

Getting hauled off the ice like an invalid only added insult to injury. Not even the crowd's support could ease his wrath against the meathead who'd taken him down. He strained to see past the EMT's hold on the gurney. Murtagh sat in the penalty box, his arrogant gaze triumphant even as his coach tore him a new asshole from over his shoulder.

Pissed, Mac pointed and mouthed, "You're mine." Then they were in the hallway heading toward the dressing room and his adrenaline waned, leaving him drawn and listless. The knee throbbed, pressing uncomfortably against his protective padding. His shoulder ached from smashing into the wall and his insides jiggled like a bowl full of jelly. But if Doc gave him the go-ahead he could still make the third period. He needed to get out there and support his team, dammit.

Coach was waiting when he arrived, pacing and

muttering while running a hand over his thinning pate. The second the EMTs set him down on the exam table Coach was breathing in his face.

"What the hell, Wanowski? I told you to pass! This superhero complex of yours is costing the team. Now what are we supposed to do, huh? We're already two men down and play-offs are coming up. Your actions tonight might have cost us the season. How do you feel now, asshole?"

Like shit, thanks for asking. The man had it in for him ever since Mac hooked up with his daughter for one never-to-be-repeated night, and nothing he did for the team was enough. It bothered him that this time Coach was right—he'd screwed up. Not that he could admit it, especially with all the interested ears wagging in the room. So, he said nothing.

The coach threw up his hands and stormed out of the room, heading back to what was left of the game. Mac just hoped they could retain their five-three lead until it ended.

"You like playing with fire, don't ya?" Doc Edwards shook his head. "Your contract is almost up with the WarHawks, Mac. Have you given any thought to what comes next?"

Mac frowned at the doc's back as he turned away to open his medical bag. "You hear something you want to tell me about?" He'd given three of his best years to this team. If the franchise planned to trade him off, the least they could do was tell him to his face.

Doc held up his hand. "Don't get your shorts in a knot, kid. I merely meant you can't play hockey forever. You must have a backup plan, right?'

Kid. Mac grunted as the other man loosened the ties on his knee guard. The resulting relief was quickly replaced by agony as blood rushed to the injury. He clenched his fists against the cool metal of the exam table and stared at the ceiling with its ugly track lighting while Doc poked and prodded the area like a sadist.

No, he didn't have a backup plan—this was it for him. Hockey was in his blood. It fed his dark soul and gave him the only true joy he'd ever known.

He couldn't leave the game.

"How bad, Doc?" He tipped his head to look down the length of his body and swore. Just as he'd thought, the knee was swollen and already showing signs of bruising. Last time he'd injured it, he'd ended up with water under the kneecap and had to have it drained. Fun times.

Edwards snapped an ice pack into action and set it against his skin before meeting his worried gaze. "I won't know for sure until we do x-rays. My best guess is your ACL." Mac winced. "Hopefully it's a sprain instead of a full tear which would mean surgery and months of rehab."

Christ, just what he didn't need right now. He laid down and covered his eyes with his forearm. "And if it's a sprain?"

"Sorry, Mac. You're still looking at two-to-four weeks recovery time, physio, and preferably crutches. I know someone, Sam Walters, who's good at this sort of injury. I'll call and see what I can get lined up."

Mac let him drone on with his voice of doom, meanwhile inside his stomach twisted into their own disastrous knots.

What was he going to do now?

Pick up your copy today!

ABOUT THE AUTHOR

JACQUIE BIGGAR is a USA Today bestselling author of Romantic Suspense who loves to write about tough, alpha males and strong, contemporary women willing to show their men that true power comes from love.

She is the author of the popular Wounded Hearts series and has just started a new series in paranormal suspense, Mended Souls.

She has been blessed with a long, happy marriage and enjoys writing romance novels that end with happily-ever-afters.

Jacquie lives in paradise along the west coast of Canada with her family and loves reading, writing, and flower gardening. She swears she can't function without coffee, preferably at the beach with her sweetheart. :)

Sign up now to keep up with Jacquie's new releases, excerpts, giveaways, and more:

Newsletter

jacqbiggar.com

jbiggar@jacqbiggar.com

ALSO BY JACQUIE BIGGAR

WOUNDED HEARTS SERIES

Tidal Falls

The Rebel's Redemption

Twilight's Encore

The Sheriff Meets His Match

Summer Lovin'

Wounded Hearts Box Set

Maggie's Revenge

With This Heart

MENDED SOULS SERIES

The Guardian

The Beast Within

GAMBLING HEARTS

Hold 'Em

Crazy Little Thing Called Love

My Girl

Married to The Texan- Box set

BLUE HAVEN

Sweetheart Cove

SINGLE TITLES

Silver Bells

The Lady Said No

My Baby Wrote Me A Letter

Tempted by Mr. Wrong

Valentine: A Hearts and Kisses Romance

Mistletoe Inn

Skating on Thin Ice